Beauty in the Beast and other musings

J.G. Barrie

For a special brother who will soon be publishing his poetry

DEDICATION

To Lea, David and Eva, who have encouraged me from their early childhood to tell entertaining stories.

ACKNOWLEDGMENTS

Edited by A. Twidale

Thanks to Katie and Marius for their help and advice.

jgb

Table of Contents

Beauty in the Beast and other musings

Beauty in the Beast

Not twenty yards away he saw the beast. A gigantic brown head with eyes glaring at him as it approached, massive jaws open, revealing fangs which made pitchforks look like toothpicks. He hoped it was not considering him as an early dinner. At six foot two and two hundred and thirty pounds, few things bothered Walter, but this was different. Very different. A feeling of terror he had never had, even as a child when confronted by a neighbourhood bully.

"Don't worry, he just looks scary, but he's very friendly," she said.

"I don't think he'll fit in the car," Walter protested, backing away from the advancing threat, "we need to get your truck."

"Nonsense! There's lots of room in the back," said Gabi as she opened the door and coaxed the one hundred and thirty-pound bullmastiff cross onto the back seat. Walter looked warily in the rear view mirror at the drooling beast behind him and wished that he had said a loving goodbye to his parents before he had left that morning. He started his 74 Jetta which lurched forward with the engine protesting under the new load, uncertain if it could complete the journey from High River to Okotoks.

And that was the beginning of Charlie's trip to a loving home where he would be the biggest, most spoiled member of the family. We had other dogs at that time: Mandy the Border Collie cross who had tattooed my right thigh a few weeks after being invited to our home; Fluffer, who loved bones (especially when they were still part of a living human's leg); Mollie, the cutest little Shitzu-cross who ever lived; and Oldie, a very frail and gentle black Lab who was on her last legs. Oh, by the way, we also had three children who

1

blended in well with the pack and even sat when we told them to! I forget their names but we had two girls and a boy (or was it two boys and a girl?). Not sure where they are now. They may have been adopted out…

But Charlie was like no other. It appeared that many mistakes were made when he was created. Perhaps he was supposed to be a camel, but the good Lord changed his mind and only gave him the gait of a camel, and the height. When he released foul smelling gas it would be enough to wilt the hardiest poplar. At this point Catherine Deneuve comes to mind; my childhood fantasy is just another old fart now. Catherine was pushing Chanel No. 5, but she should have been advertising the popular perfume called 'Charlie'. I often thought that I should have bottled Charlie's real odour and sent it to Revlon to pass on to her. Wouldn't that have been a gas?

Charlie's coat was brindle, an odd colour but very appropriate for an odd dog. His ears were like large black spades. The skin from his mouth hung loosely and flapped around as he trotted, splashing drool on anyone, or anything, within a radius of five feet. Baseball mitts were likely modeled after his large ungainly paws, which thudded across our floor whenever mealtime was announced. And, of course, he was always the first to tuck into the tub of dog food with a king sized portion, leaving half a tub of drool in its place. What he lacked in looks, he made up for with his personality.

Those who got to know him were charmed by his puppy-like behaviour. He clambered onto the couch, and would displace anyone who had been sitting there. He could be affectionate but sometimes his affection would turn to genuine love. I recall when my teenage son, what's-his-name, had his friends over to watch TV. One of them, Fred, happened to be lying on the floor and suddenly found Charlie becoming too affectionate, even though he had been fixed (not Fred…<u>Charlie</u>).

Charlie was very gregarious and would sometimes knock people over when he pushed himself through a crowd. (Silly people! They should have been more careful! Why would they not pay attention to an elephant in the room?) Any food left unattended would quickly disappear into his cavernous mouth. In its place would be a large puddle of icky, sticky, slimy *yuck*, leaving no doubt as to the identity of the thief, despite the innocence in his large brown eyes when he was chastised. At parties his wagging tail would often send glasses of Pinot Noir flying across the room. Maybe he thought that was how you aerated wine. He was not a true connoisseur…

But Charlie did have his fears. His greatest fear was the sound of thunder and the explosion of fireworks on New Year's Eve. After the first clap of thunder, he would pant heavily and frantically try to open a closet so that he could hide from the deafening noise. Often he would accidentally close himself behind the door of a room, and later try to chew his way out once the thunder had dissipated. We replaced three doors during his lifetime. One slightly chewed door in our bedroom remains as a memorial to Charlie.

But one could feel safe next to Sir Charles. Other dogs and people would give wide berth to his owner when she walked him. There were no rednecks cursing Gabi for her stand against rodeos when Charlie was around. They would become chicken-hearted and pigeon-toed when confronted with the low, rumbling growl of the Hound from Hades. Of all the dogs we have owned, Gabi felt safest with Charlie.

But the years were not kind to our Charles. His big, but weak heart, could no longer pump much needed blood to his distant extremities. His joints ached with the massive load of his body. Stairs were now insurmountable. His walks became shorter and less frequent, until he was able to walk no more. In the last week he was unable to stand. Gabi slept by his side in the living room, and we both had to lift him with a bedsheet to take him out to do his business. Charlie ate less and less, but his tail still wagged, weakly, but not for as long.

It was bright and sunny on Thursday, June 16, 2005 when I got the call from Gabi. Before she could speak I knew what she was going to say:

"I think he is going…"

It was close to noon when I left the office. I drove home reminiscing about Charlie the Clown, Charlie the Character but mostly Charlie the unforgettable Companion dog who rescued me on bad days. Why did he have to go so early? There were so many gophers to chase (and not catch), so many squirrels to bark at, and so many fields and flower beds to romp in. But like many good things, a good dog's life must also end.

My Reliant wagon, so familiar to Charlie, pulled onto the driveway. On any other day it would have been a happy scene. A woman seated on the front lawn lovingly caressing her dog, beneath the boughs of a large blue spruce tree sheltering a family of chickadees. Charlie lifted his head when I arrived and wagged his tail. But this time I was not happy to see him, because I knew that he would be leaving us soon. Very soon. His breathing slowed and soon he lay still.

That beautiful beast! As large as life, but a life no more. I couldn't hear the chickadees in the spruce tree above him. Perhaps they had stopped singing out of respect for this big-hearted animal whose soul was now rising

3

past them to disappear into the ether and from my ephemeral past. A past so brief, but yet so joyful.

Later in that month of June I looked up and saw that storm clouds had quickly gathered to block the bright sun that had shone earlier that afternoon. Rain began to fall. Large tear drops fell from the heavens. Lightning flashes briefly washed out the blues, yellows and reds of the profusion of flowers in our garden. Hail began to fall with the anger and intensity so typical of Alberta summer storms; first like pebbles and then like pigeon's eggs. The daisies, delphiniums and dahlias were shredded into tiny shards like coloured glass. All things big and beautiful now lay buried in ice, water and mud.

But I had noted that the thunder, once loud and powerful, was now far more muted, and more distant. Only a low murmur, instead of a loud clap. Perhaps there was a loving family up there in Heaven who was caring for Charlie, as he tried to creep into a quiet corner in the clouds, where the only sounds were the fluttering wings of the angels.

As You Sow

We were called botanists at one time, but you still see us as those 'tree-huggers'. Those who go into the bush and collect samples of worthless weeds to study. I was to graduate in a few weeks and had just received an offer of employment from the premier 'agri' company in the world. Genetically modified foods, I was convinced, had fed our growing population by increasing crop yields, minimizing plant disease and controlling weeds and pests.

It was my fourth year at the University of Colorado. My major was Plant Biotechnology. In preparation for my final exams I had just returned from the university library with supplemental text books that provided more information than my regular course books. I spread the contents of my knapsack onto my desk at home. *Hello what's this?* In between all the books I found a handwritten journal. It could have belonged to some other student who may have stuck it among the books inadvertently. *"H.J. Deutschendorf Jr"* was written on the inside page with the characters carefully formed, as if by a calligrapher. I skimmed through the pages and stopped at one that said:

Jan 1961: Daddy made history. Flew the plane with a peak speed of 1061 mph! Wowie! A world record. If that doesn't get the Ruskies to shit in their pants nothing will!

I flipped back a few pages:

June 1954: Got a gift from Oma. I always wanted this. Mum always tells me to go play with the kids in the block, but I don't want to tell her that they don't like me. Maybe it will be different now that I have this treasure.

July 1959. So daddy was real mad! But then how could I explain that it may be his fault too? We've moved so often that I don't have a chance to make real friends. Last week I just wanted to get away from those jerks at school so that's why I drove his car to L.A.

Freedom is when your hair is blown back as you barrel along at a hundred and twenty miles an hour! But shit, I'm grounded now.

March 1968: Met a chick today with eyes so green, and deep like the ocean. Her chestnut brown hair framed a face as pretty as the butterfly outside my window. I've got to ask her out. But she seems to be the type of girl who likes hippies or rock stars. She'll probably say "no" but maybe she'll be impressed if I write a poem for her.

It looked like the journal writer did have poetic tendencies. As I thumbed through later pages of the journal his writing had matured:

1972

> *Now he walks in quiet solitude, the forest and the streams, seeking grace in every step he takes. His sight is turned inside himself, to try and understand the serenity of a clear blue mountain lake.*

And another poem in 1975:

> *For though we are strangers in your silent world, to live on the land, we must learn from the sea. To be true as the tide, and free as a wind swell, joyful and loving, in letting it be.*

And then our poet appeared to unleash a monster within. The handwriting skewed hard right, as his pen screeched across the paper, to capture the anger and fury that boiled within him.

1982: She wants to divorce me! So I like to drink now and then. And I told her about Sally and Penny. What's the big deal? Everyone likes to drink and fool around! My God. I can still feel her delicate throat between my calloused fingers as I tried to stop those outbursts. Then I saw the wedding ring on the counter and stopped. I went outside and started the chainsaw, brought it inside and cut our bed in half. That really scared her! How could I have done that to someone I love so much? What kind of man have I become? Do I deserve to live after doing what I did to her?

I moved towards the end of the journal. The handwriting was now well formed as it had been at the beginning of the journal. The anger had dissipated.

October 11, 1997: Tomorrow I'll fly again in my new plane even though my license has been suspended due to another DUI. Shit, how do those guys catch me every time? They must park outside the bar. But when I'm up there I have no cares, no worries. I'm a lone eagle, drifting in the wind. The only sound is the air whispering past the wings.

I closed the book. I felt guilty about reading about someone's private struggles. Too much of a distraction for me when the exams were to start on Monday. I had to study, so I went back to reading the books I had borrowed from the library. What I had gleaned from these was not in the course material. Instead I learned that a popular herbicide was likely killing off Milkweed which is the main food for Monarch butterflies. Was it intentional that my professors were downplaying the harm that this caused to our environment? Could my university be favouring the big companies in the agri business? Was I being given only one side of the story, while I was being taught at this prestigious institution, which may have received corporate donations?

A few days later, I took the books back to the library and showed the librarian the journal that I had accidentally taken.

Her face lit up. "Oh! Thank you so much! What a relief! We've been looking all over for it since it was loaned to us. It's his original journal which is from the State Museum."

"But it belongs to a guy name H.J. Deutschendorf, Jr. Was he a poet or something?" I asked.

"You mean you don't know who he is? Go home and Google it. You are in for a big surprise," she said as she carefully examined the journal for any damage I may have done to this treasure.

After my exams were over, I remembered what the librarian had suggested regarding that mysterious journal writer. I typed 'H.J. Deutschendorf' in the Google Search bar. The librarian was correct. I was very surprised. A familiar face with a wide smile gazed back at me. But I was shocked to read that his aircraft had plummeted into the ocean off Pacific Grove, California, the Butterfly Town, where the Monarchs spend winter.

The tune and the lyrics echoed in the walls of my mind, as I looked into his eyes, bright and lively, as when he had written these words:

And I wonder if the smell of morning's faded, what happened to the robin's song, that sparkled in the sky? Where's all the water gone, that tumbled down the stream? Will I ever catch, another butterfly?

There was a connection between the Monarch and the writer of this song. They both made our spirits soar with them over the Blue Ridge Mountains, across the hidden valleys and the secret pathways in the enchanted forest. They stilled our souls after long tiring days. They gave us solace, in the garden, in times of sorrow. Perhaps in tribute, the butterflies annual journey ends near the *sleepy blue ocean*, beneath the gentle waves where his remains have lain since October 12, 1997.

I looked again at the Corporation's offer of employment. It was indeed a generous one, but my choice was for the Monarch.

John Denver would have wanted it so.

Author's Note: the 'poems' are the lyrics from John Denver's songs. Copyright symbol was not included to keep the reader guessing.

A Murder of Crows

"I need a team here right away. The Middle Wood area, just off the M60. It's a small barn near Leigh Road just outside the city. They'll see my white car parked on the road."

The victim had purple welts on his face. His eye sockets were puffed up and it looked like his nose was broken. Blood had trickled down his mouth and lay in a puddle by his battered face. It was a familiar sight for me after spending over thirty years with the Manchester Police Department. After so many years I was conditioned to sights like this. It didn't bother me anymore and never would. Earlier in my career I had thought about changing jobs, but never made a serious attempt, since my closest friends were the boys at the station. Couldn't think of not seeing their ugly faces every day knocking back a pint, while the grease from the bangers and mash ran down their chins. Staple food for us guys in the force.

The crime scene team arrived in two cars. They were from the closest precinct and I didn't know any of them. "In the barn?" one of them asked. He introduced himself as McAllister from the Warrington station.

"Yes," I said as he put on his overalls and plastic shoe protectors. His colleagues followed him in, pulling on their latex gloves and their masks. Later, I watched dispassionately as the victim was carried away on a gurney and loaded into the back of a mortuary van. In the distance I could hear dogs barking and the sound of horns. Several men on horses looked towards us and then looked back at their prey, or what remained of it, after the dogs had ripped it to shreds. *Another fox hunt* I thought, *sport for the idle rich. Brutal bunch of criminals. To think that my taxes goes to pay for their lordships and their bloody hobbies.*

The crew came out of the barn and removed their masks and gloves. "Blunt force trauma. No weapon nearby. Did you see anything else when you got here?" asked McAllister.

"No. I didn't. I did look in the barn and near the doors and all around but couldn't find anything."

"Who tipped you off?" he asked.

"I was passing by and a woman waved me down to say they had seen someone suspicious lurking around the barn. He didn't appear to be a local and ducked into the barn as soon as she had seen him."

"Oh! So it was lucky that you stopped by and found him. Whoever beat him up must have been from the neighbourhood."

"Why do you think so?" I asked.

"Well the only tracks leading to the barn were from your own vehicle. Unless someone had beaten him before and dumped him here."

"Could be," I said, as I followed them to the road. "I had searched for ID in his wallet but didn't find anything."

"He looks familiar. Even though his face is badly bashed in. Have to look up Missing Persons I guess. Cheerio." McAllister said, as they drove away.

My business was done. Back at the station, I filled out the report stating that the victim had no papers on him at the time of his death. I wrote that I assumed that whoever had murdered him had taken his wallet. *Type of weapon used:* 'unknown'. I wrote the date and time, signed it, and gave the report to the Duty Officer.

That afternoon I was at my desk reviewing my case load which was not as high as it should have been at this time of the year. Perhaps the street criminals were now moving to internet scams with all the easy pickings on the web from the old people.

"Benson!" Staff Sergeant Andrew Young called me into his office and closed the door. He asked me to be seated opposite him as he put on his glasses and read my report. Other than the grey hair and three stone he had gained in the last fifteen years, there was little else that had changed about him. He had been my father's partner in the Force when I was a teenager.

I will never forget the day he had come to our home to tell us that dad had been killed in the line of duty. While making an arrest of a drug dealer, dad had been slashed in the throat and died at the scene. Young had stayed the rest of the evening with us, while my mother had wept uncontrollably. I was in shock and had tried to console my dear mother. Constable Andrew Young had also wept. He had carried a heavy burden since then, because he had believed he could have prevented that from happening, but did not react fast enough. Watching my father die in his arms had burned an indelible memory in his brain. He then felt a duty towards us and had helped me join the police. He had often given me guidance as I rose through the ranks in the CID, which I later joined. We were a close bunch. As thick as thieves. A funny expression when referring to the police. But it was true. We would never let down our partners and would never betray them either. And God help those who ever killed a constable.

"Tell me Benson. Were you the first on the scene?"

"Yes sir," I said.

"How were you alerted that someone was in the barn?"

"A woman on the road."

"You mean you were just driving by and she stopped you near the barn?"

"Yes sir. But I didn't get her name. I would recognize her if I were to see her again."

"Normally I would stay in the car if someone suspicious was lurking around and then would radio for help. You know it isn't safe for you to leave your car without calling for backup first, don't you? You only had your baton and he may have been carrying a gun."

I hesitated. He was right. Our procedures had obviously been broken.

"Also, I got a call from the Crime Scene people. They said there appeared to be a scuffle in the barn and that the man was beaten to death but no weapon was found. They also mentioned this morning that the DNA check was completed and that the victim is none other than Keith McMahon, the escaped pedophile who had also murdered his wife and daughter."

"McMahon?" I asked.

"Yes, that's the man."

He took off his spectacles, sighed and looked out of the window. The poppies were blooming in the ditches in the meadow and crows were squawking their heads off on a nearby apple tree. Likely they were training their young to fly and warning them of dangers that lay ahead. The Chief was still looking in the distance, past the poppies and without turning to me said:

"Benson. There is one thing the crew did not notice."

"What was that sir?"

The Chief turned to me and said:

"Your bruised knuckles."

I looked down and covered my hands but it was too late. The old man knew.

"Benson. We have a justice system that still works. Don't do that again."

Seeing Red

Here they are again. There's no peace in the house with them. I hate them. I wish they would die.

"Wake up!" she yelled.

"You can't lie around all day. You'll never amount to anything you loser!" he shouted.

They seldom left me alone. I wished they would just go away. I have been with them since I was fourteen years old. In all those years, never once have they said anything kind to me. It's always been criticism, coercion and threats. I've tried to run away but it's no use. They find me wherever I go.

"You need to pick up some groceries you lazy bum. We have to eat you know. All you ever do is think of yourself. Day in and day out. It's you. Always you. You never think about us!" she screamed.

I stretched, put on my jeans and said nothing. It was no use talking to them. It never worked. They never stopped, no matter what I said to them. I wished they would go somewhere far. Really far. Like Inuvik. No, that would be too close...

"Get moving!"

"OK, OK." I finally muttered and left the house.

It was nice to be outside where the tulips were blooming. Large red ones. That's my favourite colour. When I was younger I would always leave the red *Smarties* for the last. Didn't every kid? Unfortunately, I had company. They had been following me. Wanted to make sure I wouldn't dilly dally, I guess.

"That's the one," he said.

A woman was coming towards me. She saw that I was gazing at the tulips and smiled at me.

"Grab her!" he said.

I didn't want to, but they both started screaming at me.

"She's the one. That's her. She was in our house last night with a knife. You've got to kill her now, before she does something!" I hesitated. She was no threat, just a nice lady going on an errand. What had they seen that I hadn't?

"The knife is in her purse. Get yours. Do it now, before it's too late!" I took a deep breath. "Do it now you coward. You've always been a yellow livered punk. You're a loser! Big time!" He shouted.

"Yeah, after all we did for him. Look how he's turned out. Why not kill yourself instead dummy? Do you want us to do it instead? Do it now, or get out of our lives!"

I reached into my jeans pocket and removed my pocket knife. I didn't want to do it. But they had told me that they saw her in our house last night when I was asleep. They never seemed to sleep. Maybe the woman was going to attack me as she passed. I opened the blade behind my right hip so that she couldn't see. She still had a smile on her face as she walked closer.

"Now! Do it now!" They both screamed. "She's reaching for it in her purse!" They were right. She did have her hand in her purse so I moved quickly and stabbed her until she fell. She began to scream. But then someone yelled.

"You bastard! What have you done? Get away from her!" I felt a blow on the back of my head and fell onto the sidewalk. A few moments later I heard police sirens approaching. I couldn't get up but I could see the tulips. Red. I looked at my hand. It was red too. *Funny*, I thought. *How did that happen?*

"What's your name?" he asked. I was now in a small room. The others had left me. The man seated opposite me was in a blue business suit with a red tie. Red again. I love that colour. I tried to touch his tie but he moved away. "Hey! Listen to me. What's your name?" he asked.

I opened my mouth but couldn't answer. I wanted to grab his red tie. It was so bright. Like those tulips. I wished I could see them again. I rose from the chair to be closer to his red tie.

"Sit down," the man ordered. I sat, wondering why he was talking to me. Who was he, and why did he bring me here? Had I been kidnapped? But why by a man in a red tie? He had tied the knot incorrectly. How could he do that with such a beautiful tie? I reached over the table and tried to adjust it for him but he slapped my hand away, got up, and left. The door closed before I could get to it.

A woman came in through the same door and asked me to sit down. But she wasn't wearing red. She was very pretty. Dark eyes and black hair. I inhaled her perfume deeply. I was reminded of red roses. I was in heaven. Maybe she was an actress. But why would she visit me here? Wherever 'here' is.

"Hello," she said. "My name is Caroline. What's yours?" She held out her hand, which I took. It was so soft. She was so gentle. I hadn't met someone like her before. She seemed to like me. Once again I opened my mouth to say something but suddenly they were in the room with me.

"Kill her. Before she gets you. She's a bitch. Don't trust her." I started to move towards her but the door opened again. Two men entered and pushed me down onto the chair. The beautiful woman, Caroline, was not surprised by my attempt to get closer to her. I guess many men had tried to do that before. Maybe that was why she had bodyguards. They now pressed down on my shoulders and stood behind me.

"I was asking. What is your name young man?" she asked, with that gentle smile.

"Charles." I answered, before the others could answer on my behalf. They were quiet now, probably afraid of the bodyguards. They said nothing but they were breathing heavily. This was new to them too. I wished they would run away from me now.

"Do you know why you are here Charles?" she asked.

"No. I don't. By the way, where am I?"

"We are in a Police Station. Remember they brought you here a little while ago?"

"I don't. But why? I didn't steal anything." I said.

This was weird. A police station of all places. But why was such a beautiful woman in a police station with me? She started talking to me softly and I watched her lips move, but then the others started screaming again and

I couldn't hear what she was saying. I put my hands over my ears so that the other two would know that I didn't want to listen to them, but they went on and on, screaming at me. Threatening me. Telling me that I was a useless piece of shit to get caught. My beautiful Caroline took my hand in hers and I suddenly felt a sting on my arm. Her angelic face faded away as I held her hand. I remembered nothing after that.

I was now in a court house. People had screamed that I was a monster while I was being led into the courtroom. But I had done nothing. Maybe someone would understand. The judge wore black and so did the Prosecutor. But my lawyer wore a red scarf. I had asked her to wear it whenever we met. Somehow it helped me focus. To concentrate. To ignore those two people who were always screaming at me to do things that were wrong. I would tell them that it was wrong, but they wouldn't listen to me.

I think I was fifteen when that happened. I can't tell you too much about the intervening years but I am now forty years old and I have a friend. We share a room and a nice lady visits us. She puts a syringe in my arm and draws blood from it. I don't mind that. You see, my blood is red. I love that colour.

She said, "I am very pleased with your progress Charlie. Your last blood test showed that the medication is at the right level in your body. You must never forget to take it. Because if you don't take it, they'll be back in less than two weeks."

I knew who "they" were. The voices. The voices that echoed in my skull. The voices that controlled most of my actions no matter how hard I tried to ignore them. The voices that forced me to do things that I would never do otherwise. The nurse told me that I had almost killed a woman when I was younger. The voices made me to do it. The nurse told me that I am a paranoid schizophrenic. And will be one for the rest of my life. There is no cure. You see, I am not a monster. I just need my little red pills to still the voices. Hopefully for as long as I live. When I left the Alberta General Hospital in Edmonton last week to come to this group home, I heard voices again. They were screaming, shouting and cursing me:

"Bring back Capital Punishment!"

"What is our Justice System coming to with the likes of him on our streets? Who cares for our children?"

"Go back in there, you son-of-a bitch!"

The policewoman put her arm around my shoulders. "Don't worry Charlie, just ignore them. They don't know the truth about you."

My eyes adjusted to the bright sunlight. And there they were. A large group of people across the street from the hospital. It was a demonstration. They didn't want me out. The voices were not coming from within my head. They were from the other side of the street. People carrying placards. People yelling. But just behind the crowd stood a woman. She had no placard. She was not yelling. Our eyes met. She understood. She had been my victim. I could have been her son.

I am not a monster. I am just a very sick man.

Crossing Venus

A fly landed in his hooch but it didn't matter to old Hank. He removed it with his gnarled finger and flicked it away. No good to throw out this stuff. What a sauce it was! His daddy would have been proud of him, making hooch as good as he did. Hank's rocking chair squeaked on the old grey deck boards as he took another gulp. It was a warm afternoon like the type he and Myrtle used to enjoy here on the deck, when she was alive. But she had been gone some years now, to the big farmhouse in the sky. Hank looked at the bright yellow canola gently bending in the breeze, and he knew that crop was going to fetch him a good price this year. Other than money, he had few joys these days. One of these was watching Venus, across the fence.

Thou shall not covet... he chuckled to himself. *Hell with that! Ain't the same. Ain't never seen a piece of ass like that one.* His neighbor, Sam, had stolen his property often enough. *So all's fair in love and war.*

His rheumy eyes followed her every gyration while savouring the gentle curves of her body, as she stretched and moved slowly out of the sun, where she had been warming her velvety smooth flesh. He drooled as she got up and ambled over to the shack to get another drink, her rear end swaying deliciously in the soft sunlight.

Gawd! Ah'd love to sink my teeth into that rump! How he wanted her! Playing 'I Spy' by himself was no fun. He imagined being with someone, sipping hooch at the dinner table and enjoying Pigs in Blankets. His desire grew more intense, especially when she occasionally cast her eyes in his direction, licking her lips to arouse his hunger even more. From the living room he heard his favourite song on the old stereo *"Blue Suede Shoes"*. He picked up his gunnysack. It was time. He couldn't wait anymore. He had to have her! It was going to be a hot time in the old house tonight!

Venus headed to the dugout for a swim, in the raw. Hank jumped the fence and moved quietly through the tall grass, every muscle tensed since he knew that there was going to be a struggle. She was a feisty one. *What do you expect with a body like that!*

He drew closer, dropped his sack, and grabbed her bare rear end but she jerked backwards and Hank flipped over the edge into the deep dugout. He couldn't swim and there was no one to save his bacon. Venus looked placidly while bubbles from the dugout became smaller, signifying the end of old Hank.

Crossing Venus had been a big mistake. Venus was one smart pig...

Fifty Ways to Lose Your Readers

It was a dark and stormy night as is usual in trite stories, this one being no different. A lone pirate sloop drifted with only two persons on board, Long John Sliver and Marsha Mallow. Long John Sliver was the son of a ship's carpenter, Joseph Sliver, who was certainly not religious, like the other guy. In fact, his father had visited many unholy lands and befriended women who were not of the cloth. That was the naked truth. Whenever Long John had asked Joseph about his family tree, he only muttered that he 'was a son of a beech'. So Long John stopped asking him because he didn't want to go out on a limb…

After the dark and stormy night, at the crack of dawn, Long John was on the deck, even though he didn't have a leg to stand on. He had lost it because he was always stepping on other pirate's toes, and when you do something like that, you know you're on a slippery slope. But he had a shoe on the other foot, and walked softly and carried a big stick.

Blackbeard, one of the pirates who chose not to set sail, had warned him: "Beware the tides of March." Even Long John Sliver's first cousin, the famous Goldfinger (who, after the accident, was known as Captain Hook), had told him that "You only live once." Billy Bud and his wife, Rose, had also told him that he didn't have both oars in the water, and that he should fix his sail first. They also said that "a stitch in time saved nine." But he replied that he would not follow that thread, and he left the dock with his threadbare sails in the sunset.

"Marsha, are you there?" he called softly, as he cocked his head.

Marsha was his mate, who, figuratively speaking, was a 36-26-36, had 20-20 vision and had a 50-50 chance of getting her way with men. In other words, she could be considered a cute number, and she was number one with Long John. Her auburn curls cascaded down her snowy white shoulders even though the sun had blazed on the deck for the last two weeks. Alas, perchance she had remained too long on the poop deck. The sea affects the bowels of the ship, and also those with bowels. She had heard Long John's melancholy call, because her hearing was acute, and she could hear a pin drop, even in the ocean.

"Yes Long John, I am here. Are you pissing in the wind again? Did you fix the loose cannon, or were you asleep at the wheel?" She answered, jokingly.

Marsha came out from the poop deck and gazed at his muscles which rippled under the crimson sky. He was strong as an ox and fit as a fiddle. But he didn't have one. A fiddle, that is, and the cow had jumped over the moon (which had been an oxident).

"Marsha, Marsha, Marsha," he said, joyfully.

"Long John, Long John, Long John," she responded, warmly.

"Did you want to ask me something?" he asked attentively, as he cocked his head, for the second time.

"Do you find me attractive?" she asked, coquettishly.

He looked at her lovely lashes as she languished, laughingly on the port side, or was it the starboard side? He could never remember, since he was never dealt a full deck.

"Of course I do. You know it. You are cute as a button," he responded, immediately, as he cocked his head. Hopefully for the last time.

"They say, that beauty is in the eye of the beholder, Long John," she said flirtingly, "but I know you will always protect me, come hell or high water."

"Hiawatha died a long time ago," replied Long John, unthinkingly.

"No, no, that's not what I said. But never mind. Did you get forty winks last night?" asked Marsha, wearily.

"Not really, it rained cats and dogs," he said, gloomily.

"Oh? By the way, what happened to the ship's cat?" she asked, questioningly.

"Dead," he responded, quickly.

"Dead, how?" she asked, sadly.

"You know, Marsha," he replied, dejectedly.

"I don't, please tell me Long John," she asked, pleadingly.

"Curiosity killed the cat," he answered, grimly.

"Well maybe we should get a dog," she suggested, smartly, always a step ahead.

"We already had two. Don't you remember? They died." He stated, disconsolately.

"How?" she asked, inquisitively.

"They got into a fight. You should have seen the fur fly. And then it was dog eat dog," he stated, ruefully.

They spent the rest of the day chewing the fat and making waves. Late that evening they went into the dining quarters.

"Let's have dinner Long John. Your goose is cooked, but the last time you said it didn't cut the mustard," she said, accusingly.

"I couldn't stomach that, but did I hurt your feelings Marsha?" he asked, caringly.

"You did, Long John. It cut like a knife," she said, sharply.

"Boy, did I have egg on my face, but I got my just desserts. I could have been chopped liver, and you could have rubbed my nose in it. But then, you should have taken it with a grain of salt," he replied, abashedly.

"I'll cook something else next time. There's plenty of fish in the ocean," she said, sardine-occly.

They finished dinner. "I'm tired now, let's hit the sack," he said, suggestively.

"But it's too early," she responded, teasingly.

"Early to bed early to rise, they say," he said, wisely.

In bed they snuggled together like birds of a feather. (They also flock together.)

"Long John, there's something I need to ask you," she remarked, tenderly.

"What Marsha?" he asked, lovingly.

"Are you gay?" she questioned, impertinently.

"Yes, I'm happy and gay," he answered, ingeniously.

"You can say that again," she said, merrily.

"Yes, I'm happy and gay," he repeated, funnily.

"Well, in that case we can just be fair weather friends," she remarked, appropriately.

"Long John, there's something else," she stated, worriedly.

"What Marsha?" he asked, inquiringly.

"We can't go on like this," she said, adroitly.

"Why not?" he asked, quizzically.

"Because very soon, there'll be blood on our hands," she said, fearfully.

"Why?" he asked, anxiously.

"When all is said and done," she said, prophetically, "someone's going to kill the guy who wrote this."

If He Could See You Now

How lucky he had been to find the perfect place to live on his own for the first time. The elderly owners of the home had been hesitant to rent the suite to him initially, but after they spoke to his parents they agreed. The Pattersons had left for the Lake prior to the long weekend in June and Steve enjoyed the solitude he had so longed for. He was proud he had rented a place of his own, despite his parent's pleadings to put it off until later. They felt that it was perhaps too soon to leave their home. He still had so many more things to learn before moving out, they had told him.

He heard every gurgle, gasp and sputter of the Spirit River as it snaked through forests and nourished life along its meandering path. Steve sipped his tea and listened to robins, blue jays and sparrows, as they joined in a noisy chorus to celebrate the bright morning. The scent of lilacs and lavender wafted into his basement suite, mingling with the aroma of his freshly brewed tea.

"Too soon..." he smiled to himself. He was sixteen years old and had just graduated. How can his dear mum and dad feel it was "too soon?" But he knew that without their encouragement he would never have finished high school, would never have learned to play the piano, and would never have been able to read. Reading had opened a bright new world for him and his reading of classic fiction and non-fiction had helped him graduate with good marks in school. Although he did well in Science and Math, English literature was his favourite subject and he planned to take up Fine Arts and Music at the University.

"What should I do today in my new digs?" he asked himself.

Steve had specifically requested mum and dad not to visit him on this day. He had wanted to clean up and rearrange the furniture by himself after they had helped him move in. They would then get a pleasant surprise when he invited them for tea and cake as a special housewarming. He had learned how to bake and had made his own bread and pastries using recipes from his mother. He helped himself to another cup of freshly steeped

Darjeeling tea. *Damn, that's a fine brew* he thought. He had experimented with different kinds of tea and had become a connoisseur of fine blends which greatly amused his father, Ken Brown, whose own father had run a tea plantation in Darjeeling in the early 1900's. He recalled, when he was about five years old, Grandpa had said: "Stevie, smell each set of these leaves. This is tea. The leaves smell different and look different, but they all come from the same plant whether it's green, black, white or oolong tea."

He learned that the difference was the amount of air these were exposed to after being picked. He often drank tea, but liked the occasional coffee much to the dismay of grandpa. Premium coffees from Africa were a treat for him since these released mysterious flavours from the 'dark continent' he intended to visit. In his boyhood dreams, he would swing from the vines with Tarzan and the apes, and participate in dangerous rescues of endangered tigers being attacked by mean white hunters in khakis and solar *toupees*.

As he took a sip of tea, rain started to rustle the leaves of the tree in the front yard. The boughs of the birch creaked and groaned with each gust of wind. Large drops thrummed on the roof and seemed to grow louder and louder, demanding entrance to his newly rented suite. His cell phone summoned him with *The Eagles* melody *Peaceful Easy Feeling*.

"Stevie. Is it raining hard over there?" asked Patricia, his mother.

"Quite a bit," replied Steve.

"Do you need any help? I can send your father over. The forecast is for heavy rainfall to continue and I am quite worried about the area you are living in, since it is in a flood plain."

Steve smiled at this ruse to check on him on his first day away from home. He was in a town at least half an hour from the city his parents lived in. *Just the right distance to maintain his independence* he thought.

"I'm fine mum. The house hasn't flooded yet but if it does I'll ask my neighbour Noah to help." He told her that he would be prepared for any eventuality and would call if he needed help. He smiled, shook his head and hung up.

It rained all night while Steve sat on the couch reading *The Last Juror*. He hadn't read John Grisham previously and quite liked the way this book was written. He took the book to bed and later fell asleep as rain continued to pound on the roof.

He awoke the next morning fully refreshed. He filled the coffee-maker with water, added his Kenyan Mountain Blend to the paper filter and pressed the Start button, and awaited the aroma of freshly made coffee to burst out from the fine grind. He took his mug out of the shelf, reached for the sugar on the left side of the cabinet, and grabbed a teaspoon from the drawer below. Outside there was no birdsong, only the sound of the river. No sounds came from the busy street outside and no smell of freshly brewed coffee.

Darn. The electricity must be off. It was then that he noticed his slippers were wet. *Oh no! The rain must have leaked through the door last night.*

He opened the door and water gushed into the room and angrily swirled into the living area. Steve lost his balance and was pulled onto the deck and then down the slope, into the alley and past the fence which had been washed away. He couldn't tell where he was, as the raging current swept him farther away. Fence boards, garbage cans and branches hammered his body while he struggled to breathe in the violent eddies. He tried to grab any large objects to stay afloat but was pulled down again.

Don't panic he thought, having remembered his swimming lessons when he was a young boy. *If you can't swim, float on your back.* And that is what he did when he broke the surface. The torrent of water pulled him along faster and faster and he appeared to be in the middle of the river. He felt the warmth of his mother's embrace as he heard her whispering softly in his ear. "You can do it Stevie. You can do it." Waves crashed around him and he thought he had heard voices. "Help!" he called out while the waves battered his body.

"Grab the pole!" someone shouted.

He was pulled under water again but forced himself to surface a few moments later. Steve heard a motor approaching and more voices.

"Grab the pole son!"

He reached out but couldn't find it.

"He can't hear," someone said.

The boat moved closer to him and someone had grabbed his hand, then his waist and he was on board.

"Are you cold young man?" A woman asked as she handed him a blanket.

"Just a little bit," he said, through teeth that chattered more from fear than from cold. He draped the blanket around himself.

"You are a very lucky man. You almost got sucked away. You were so close to the boat! Why didn't you grab the pole which my wife held out to you?" the man asked.

Steve removed the blanket and turned to his rescuer.

"I couldn't. You see, I'm blind."

Resurrection

It was late Saturday evening and I had been totally engrossed in my next project. But the ideas were not flowing as they normally would on a cool moonlit night, when I would have expected that perhaps a touch of lunar madness would have increased my creativity. I was alone at home for a change, my wife having gone to tend to a sick friend. The midnight hour was approaching but I was not tired enough. I felt that a brisk walk in the cool night air would stimulate my creative juices, or perhaps tire me enough to assure a sound sleep.

My loyal companion, George, a German Shorthair Pointer, looked at me inquiringly with his chocolate brown face, ears raised in anticipation of an adventure. He jumped off our (his) well used couch when he saw me at the door, shook the remains of what was once a tail, while his large brown eyes pleaded that I should take him along as I often did.

The air had an invigorating bite and the moon loomed large over the eastern horizon painting the pathway with its silvery shafts of light. The green fingers of tulip bulbs poked impatiently from the loam, testing the air above, and sending quiet messages to awaken them sooner into flower.

As I closed the door, a large owl turned its head. The ivory eyes demanded why I would disturb the stillness of this magical night. It shifted nervously on the bough of a spruce tree, shaking off a cloud of snow still clinging to the branches from the morning's snowfall. George looked up, catching flecks of powder on his snout. He decided that the owl was less interesting than the squirrel, a frequent visitor that provided far more stimulation. The owl's gaze followed us as we turned the path into the wooded glade. It likely continued its vigil for an adventurous or itinerant mouse.

Man, and Man's best friend, walked the lonely path along the riverbank. I let George off his leash so that he could follow his nose which would pick up the minutest trace of mice, gophers or voles which may be scurrying for food on this grand night for dining. The river gurgled by, reminding me of a lyric in a recent song I had learned: *Flow Gently Sweet Afton*. The shiny ribbon wound its way into the blackness of the forest ahead, disappearing into the stillness of the moonlit landscape where midnight stalkers waited silently for their prey. My pace quickened as it was really quite late. Being alone in this area, at this time of the night, could attract the attention of cougars or bears, which may be early risers from their winter's sleep.

There was a soft rustling behind me and I turned to see what it was, but whatever it was, had taken shelter in the tall grass or the copse of trees behind me. I trudged on, enjoying this pleasant walk on the moon washed river bank, when a huge animal jumped out of the trees ahead of me. The large ears and eyes may have belonged to a moose, but its manner of movement was unlike any animal I had seen before. My fingers trembled at this sudden apparition and my heart may have paused briefly. My feet froze to the ground and my knees locked, disabling my escape plan which was screaming in my frenzied brain.

George stopped short, looked at the animal and quickly turned and bounded home at great speed, despite his arthritic shoulder. He did not mind leaving his loving owner and provider of food and shelter to this huge, hungry animal. I had been abandoned by my fickle companion who could possibly have been an alternate source of food for the large beast. I felt a cold hand grip my heart and slowly constrict this vital organ while the large animal moved closer to me, moonlight glinting off its sharp, protruding incisors and nose twitching, savouring the aroma of its prey. *Why must I to die on a beautiful night like this?* Thankfully, my knees gave way and I collapsed onto the cold stones of the riverbank, unconscious and waiting for my ambassador of death to do his duty. The moon lost its glow and the stars were snuffed out as I faded quickly into the blackness of the night.

When I awoke, I was in a dark confined place with a heady aroma which I recalled with joy from my early childhood years. My hands felt the smoothness of the walls but I was barely able to stand. I kept falling onto the slippery, sloping floor. Crawling in the darkness I tried to fathom this prison that I was locked in. The blackness was overwhelming but as my eyes grew accustomed to this, I saw a small crack of light. Crawling towards it, I placed my hands on what appeared to be a large smooth stone and was able to push it out with little effort. An intense white light behind it blinded me temporarily. Shielding my eyes, I took small steps. My feet sank into the soft terrain and it felt like I was walking in a large field of freshly picked cotton. My eyes had difficulty focusing in the whiteness all around me. But it was not cold and only slightly damp. Ahead was a large, dark brown arch and, under the arch, was a figure clad in what appeared to be a fur coat and a hat. I looked behind me at what had been my prison: a large egg-shaped structure. I cautiously approached the stranger assuming that this was my attacker who had now brought me to this strange place. He stood there silently gazing at me.

"Where am I?" I asked.

"Where do you think Brother John?" he asked.

"So I'm dead?" I asked. "Heart attack no doubt?"

"Yes John, you died but you have been resurrected."

"Then you must be Peter," I said knowingly.

"Yes. Peter Rabbit," he clarified. "Happy Easter" he said, smiling broadly, while moving his large ears from side to side.

"Why me?" I asked.

"Because you were kind to me and my friends by being a vegetarian."

"But what about George?" I asked. "Is he here too?"

"Yes, but he's being his usual self, chasing the Easter Bunny into Eternity."

It's Our Anniversary, eh?

So it's our anniversary. Maybe the eleventh or twelfth, I dunno but I wuz in the Dollar Store, so I says to myself: "Hey Al, son of Sal, why not get the little lady something good, eh?" I see this funny metal sign which says: *I love you so much I would dye for you. So which colour should I dye myself?* Funny, eh? I thought it wuz real funny so I take a fiver over to the cashier.

"Hey lady, I like this. It's for the ol' lady. It's our anniversary. Neat, eh? Do I give you a Loonie for this, or what?"

She gives me this look, eh? No smile, nuttin. Maybe she doesn't like me, eh? But she rings up the sale and it's $4.99. So I hesitate, but give her the fiver.

"Keep the change lady. It's our anniversary, eh?"

So she gives me this look again. And I think to myself. "Hey! What's the world comin' to, eh? Nobody thanks you for a tip anymore." So I figure. "Hey what the hell. It's our anniversary eh? So I should get the ol' lady some flowers, eh. Maybe some red ones. What the hell, let's splurge a little, it's our anniversary eh? I hope she'll like my gift. I think it's funny. *I will dye for you.* Hilarious!

So I get into my 76 Ford pickup with no tailgate. Still runs good. Change the oil myself. Every two years. Oil is expensive these days you know. But good maintenance is important, eh? She's a real beaut though. Black. I love black. It's macho to drive a black pickup, eh? I even got them truck nuts hangin' from the bumper. People see me with my tattooed arm and give me the thumbs up. They know me. I'm a good guy, eh? I have a shotgun at home and love huntin'. Got a gun rack in the back winder of the pickup. Just a regular guy, eh. That's why my ol' lady still loves me, eh. A regular guy. Put my undershirt on one arm hole at a time, eh? Wash it every two weeks to save the ol' lady some work, eh? I'm very considerate they say. That's whut the guys in the body shop tell me while we are spray paintin' them ol' pickups.

Oh, I said it wuz my anniversary, eh? So you wanna know where we got hitched right? Well it wuzn't one of them fancy Las Vegas type weddin's where an Elvis impersonator is the parson, and everyone is wearin' buckskins and cowboy boots. And blondes with pink polyester dresses, chewin' gum, tiaras in their bouffants and holdin' paper roses. No siree. No fancy stuff for me. I did it right. I did it my way!

I love my work see, so we got married in the body shop. Just outside the paint booth. With my buddies as best men, eh? They changed into clean coveralls for the ceremony, eh? Bert, the boss, he acted as the parson and read us the vows. Don't read very well but he did OK for a grade six dropout. Then the boss took pictures with my Kodak Instamatic, eh? Good camera eh? And then me and the guys and my new bride had hooch and hamburgers to celebrate. Couldn't put the BBQ in the shop, otherwise the weddin' coulda been a real blast! Hey that wuz great! The boys loved it. And we all got pissed.

Minnie used to work there and had previously shacked up with the boss, but picked me to marry instead. I apologized to Bert for stealin' his girlfriend. But he says to me:

"Son. If yew two are in love. Thet's all thet matters."

She still sees him once in a while and has a sleepover. Nuttin serious, eh. She tells me they just watch Lawrence Welk and drink beer until he passes out. To me, it's important that she keep in touch with her ol' friends eh? Why should she give them up just because she's married, eh? I don't give up beer, pizza and hockey just because I'm married, eh? I got my principles. An' she does too. Got them principles, I mean.

Got my principles from muh dad, Sal. He's a good guy y'know. Every birthday since I wuz sixteen, he brang me a six-pack as a gift. Now, how great is that, eh? I'm proud of muh dad. He's whut they call a "PI". Means "Private Eye". Makes good money, but I didn't think you could make much money as a Peepin' Tom. But then, muh dad, he's a regular guy, eh?

Anyways, where wuz I? Oh yeah. So I take the gift in a white plastic bag from the Dollar Store. They don't gift wrap you know… and I go to get some purty red flowers. She likes red. They sell red flowers at the gas station you know. The FasGas by the bridge? But on the way I pass my buddy's yard. He likes gardenin' y'know. An' I see them red flowers stickin' out of truck rims under his bay winder. Eddie's some classy guy, eh? Bay winder, truck rims. Wow. They look real fancy. Anyways, so I thought. "Would Fast Eddie mind if I took a few of them flowers?" I think they are called two lips. Nice name for a flower. Two lips. Maybe the ol' lady will like 'em, and I can plant a kiss on her two lips as I give them to her. Funny, eh? I knew you'd think that. Guys in the shop think I'm a real joker too.

Once I remember puttin' popcorn in the crapper. Wow, now that wuz funny! My shit didn't sink? Get it? My shit don't sink? Ha ha! The boss didn't like the joke so I had to clean the crapper.

Where wuz I? Yeh. So I think: should I take Fast Eddie's two lips or not? He'd prob'ly get real pissed at me. But hey, what the hell, I'll tell him it's for our anniversary, eh? So I drive the pickup on his lawn. He don't mind. He says that takes care of them dandelions. But then his missus comes out and she asks:

"Hey whaddya want? Eddie's at the bar. Wanna come in for a beer?" I look at her. She's still in her kimono. It wuz noon. I guess she must have had quite a night with Fast Eddie. But I say:

"No, can't. It's our anniversary eh."

So she says "Hey man. I can join you. I'll bring over a case of the good stuff."

I says, "No, the ol' lady wouldn't like that."

She sucks on her cigarette and says: "So whaddya goin' to do? Go out to Harveys for dinner?"

"No, run out of coupons. Maybe we'll just eat in and watch the hockey game. Flames playin' the Canucks. Can't miss that, eh? It's our anniversary. What better way to celebrate eh?"

I look at her on the lawn with them curlers in her hair, an open kimono holdin' a six pack of *Black Label* close to her cleavage, an' blowin' smoke in the wind. Maybe she and Fast Eddie will hit the town tonight. Maybe go bowlin' or play pool with the boys, eh?

Anyways, she went into the house and I couldn't take Eddie's two lips, but I saw a bunch of dandelions on the driver's side of the pickup, and I sez to myself "Myself. The old lady loves flowers. Fast Eddie hates dandelions."

So I picked up a bunch, put them under my arm, and drove home. Maybe she'd like yellow flowers too, eh? So I drive home (my dad's basement, since we're still savin' to rent our own basement suite someday) and pull out the white plastic bag with the gift, stuff it under my arm, slick my hair back, spit out my tobacco, wipe muh lips with the back of muh hand, look into the side view mirror to make damn sure I look real good for the ol' lady. Yup that's me awright, plastic bag under the arm, yellow flowers in my hand and a good feeling in my crotch.

Can't wait to see how happy the ol' lady will be that I remembered our tenth anniversary, or is it the eleventh? Ah shit, what the hell, it's our anniversary.

Happy Anniversary, eh!

It's Our Honeymoon, eh?

So where wuz I? Oh yeah. The ol' lady, y'know, Minnie, really liked the metal sign that I bought her for our anniversary.

"Hey, if you get three more you can weld them together and use it as a tailgate on the truck." She's some smart cookie, eh? Like I knew she wuz smart because she completed Junior High, eh? I didn't think that school went that far, eh? I'm glad I married 'up' as they say, y'know.

Anyways, she asked me to get some groceries. I do that sometimes, eh. So I go to the *Sobeys* store and I walk down the aisles, real casual, eh, like them housewives who know whut they are lookin' for, eh. So I stop at the aisle which says 'Condiments'. And I think, "What duz 'condiments' mean"? Is it Candy and Mints an' they spelled it wrong? But anyways in the aisle I find ketchup. Hey the price of ketchup was a dollar forty-nine for the house brand, eh? And on the shelf above they had "*Heinz 57*" for three forty-nine eh! You gotta be kiddin' me. Three forty-nine for a bottle of ketchup? Gimme a break, eh. You know why they call it *Heinz 57*? Because they tried fifty six times to get it right... an' they still don't got it right. The <u>price</u> is not right!

Anyways, so I walk into the next aisle and I see my favourite: pork and beans. The best. So I buy a dozen cans eh, maybe have a party of pork and beans and beer, eh? That should really be somethin'. Me and the boys eatin' pork and beans right from the can, eh, with them fancy white plastic spoons eh? And drinkin' beer and eatin' beans all night eh? Why not call *Heinz Baked Beans* "Heinz Farty Nine", eh? Who gives a shit about global warmin' eh? The Prime Minister once said "The govmint does not belong in the bathrooms of their citizens." And he was darn right, eh. I think his name was Trudough. French kind of name. French bread, eh? True dough, get it? I'm a real joker eh, hard to keep up with me.

Anyways, for once the Frenchies said somethin' right. Global Warmin' is another Commie conspiracy. I should know, eh. I watch out for them Commies. They tried to have a Gun Registry, eh? For long guns they said, eh. But me, I'm smart. I only have short guns, Colt 45, Walther PPK, Smith and Wesson, eh. They're short guns, eh. No need to register them, eh. Oh yeah, I do have a Remington shotgun but it's only three feet long, eh. No need to register that, eh? What the hell! I think the govmint wanted to watch out for them guys who have tanks and cannons, eh. Now <u>those</u> are long guns, eh? Can't really go huntin' for Bambi in one of them things, eh? Only if yer a Commie bastard who is tryin' to take over our Conservative land, eh. That's when I bring out my guns, eh. No Commie bastards will ever enter Alberta. But BC? Now that's OK, eh. They are Liberals, eh. Not much different. And the NDP. Now gimme a break, eh. Them guys may as well have Poutine as their leader, eh. No, that can't be his name, it's too Frenchie. Maybe Pooppin is their leader. That's what the Ruskie President's name is! Pooppin! No wonder they are in deep shit all the time, eh. Anyways I'm not a political kind of guy, eh. I'm just a regular guy. Change my underwear once a week, get a haircut if I remember, just a regular guy, eh.

Anyways, I come home with a case of pork and beans, No Name ketchup, *Doritos*, *Cheesies* and some *Coke*, eh. Just a regular guy's food, eh. Ah shit. I forgot the wieners again. Guess I'll have to go back later. But Minnie's not home, eh. So I call Bert and Minnie answers the phone.

"I'll be home in a little bit hun. Just helpin' Bert with his supper."

Now what kind of woman is that, eh? Helpin' my boss? Wow! Is she ever Mrs. Right, eh? And then again, if you can't trust your wife and your boss, who can you trust, eh? I know that relationship is what's called "Plutonic", eh. My grandpappy tole me that if there's Pluto in it, then it must be good. Y'know Bert had an accident, eh? I once asked him about it. Bert looked at Minnie, and Minnie looked at Bert, an' I tell yah them tears sprung in their eyes, and they just stood there and shook their heads. So I figured the accident hurt his privates, eh? That's why they can't talk about it, eh. And that's why they have them Privacy Laws, eh? Gotta protect your privates, eh?

Anyways, like I said, I'm just a regular guy, eh. Like most regular guys, I like to do just three things, eh. Eat, sleep and …y'know (wink, wink, nudge, nudge). Just a regular guy, eh. Ain't nuttin wrong with being a regular guy, eh.

So where wuz I? Oh yeah. I told you about my weddin' but didn't tell you about my honeymoon, eh? Well, Bert decided to come along too, eh. Really looks after us, eh. So he reserves a motel for us in Balzac, eh. Just across from the gas station.

"Yew don' wanna run out of gas on yer honeymoon, eh?"

Anyways, so me and my bride get this nice room with white sheets and real foamy pillows all puffed up. Even had a TV set and a carpet in the room, with a clean brown arborite table to put our six pack on, so it stays cool by the winder. There wuz even a closet so I could hang up my coveralls, eh? Now how fancy can you get, eh?

Anyways, so our first evenin' started off with a bang. If you know what I mean (wink, wink, nudge, nudge) and then Minnie said she had to do her hair to look extra purty for me on our honeymoon night, so she insisted that Bert help her with her hair. He was in the next room, eh. So that's where she went for a bit. Came back after an hour. Noticed her hair was all mussed up.

"Oh, that's in fashion now hun," she said.

Jeez I can never keep up with them women's fashions, eh? Bouffants, or pigtails for hair. Purple lipstick, cut offs one year, thongs the next year, really makes it hard to buy a woman somethin' when you don't know what's in fashion, eh. Anyways, where wuz I? Oh yeah.

"Bert wants to buy us dinner tonight," she says.

I said "Hey that's mighty nice of him. Where's he wanna take us?"

"Oh," she said, "the gas station has a real nice restaurant eh, so don't wear them jeans with the paint stains, eh."

So we go there for dinner, eh. Anyways, Bert wants to order us a drink to celebrate.

"What'll yew have Al?" he chuckles, "one of them Energy Drinks? *Red Bull*, eh? Or is Red Balls?"

But we end up with the usual. *Black Label*. But this time Bert asks the waitress to bring one of them fancy white plastic glasses for us to drink from, because it's a classy restaurant, eh. Can't drink from the bottle, eh. So she brings the beer and the plastic glasses, blows a bubble with her *Wrigley's Spearmint* gum and says: "The special today is a Double Cheese Burger with fries or onion rings and a large coke for two ninety-nine."

"Wow," I said, "that's good fer me."

Bert and Minnie nodded and the waitress sashayed away and called to the kitchen: "Three more burgers to burn," an' she turns around and gives me a wink, like she knew it was muh honeymoon.

Bert is what they call a cornysewer, eh? Knows how to read them fancy menus, and knows how one drinks beer real proper, eh. An' them guys from Montreal think they are cornysewers, eh. Gimme a break, eh. They can't tell the difference between a wiener an' a hot dog, eh. Besides they don't drink beer there either, eh. Just that pukey red wine in them fancy green bottles, eh. An' they even put corks in them bottles too. Would you believe, corks? No siree, they call themselves cornysewers and have never heard of screw caps on bottles, eh. I'm sure glad I wasn't born in that part of the world, eh. Drinkin' red wine all day an eatin' poutine. And those women there don' ever wear jeans, eh. Just them dresses eh, like they are goin' to get married or somethin', eh.

Anyways, where wuz I? Oh yeah, so we have our double cheese burger and a few bottles of beer, drunk from them fancy white plastic glasses, eh, an' then Bert says, "I guess I should leave yew two lovebirds alone, eh."

And he toddles off to his room. So I look at Minnie and she looks at me. So cute, with a cigarette stuck where her front tooth used to be.

"You know what hun, I'll see you in a bit. I need Bert to do my hair again so I look extra purty for you tonight."

"Go ahead hun, I'll be waitin' for ya."

And she giggles, wiggles her sweet little ass and follows Bert to his room. Now ain't I one lucky son-of-a-bitch?

It's my honeymoon, eh?

Jonboy's Complaint

I was well over the pain threshold. Not physical pain, but mental torment, which was far more severe. It had led me to the office of Dr. Angela von Burstinhead. All because Babette had taken off.

Her prim, proper and prissy receptionist lowered her spectacles and looked at me as I walked in. Miss Prissy beckoned me to be seated after I gave her my name. She asked if I would like a cup of tea, coffee or a glass of juice. I declined. With a cute smile she walked down the corridor wiggling her little Austrian ass that I had the sudden urge to pinch. It was my urges that had brought me to a shrink's office in the first place. She returned in a few moments.

"Frau Doktor vill see you now." I was led into the examination room. I read the certificate on the wall. *Diploma in Psychiatry, University of Vienna, 1974.* It had been signed and stamped by Baron von Lustinbed.

Dr. Angela came into the room, frowned at me over the rims of her spectacles, and asked me to lie on the faux leather couch. It was in the centre of her walnut paneled examination room. An original abstract oil painting hung from the wall. It was a swirling mess of brown, green and yellow which should likely have been titled:

"Artist's Intestinal Response to Spicy Legumes," or,

"Diarrhea of a Madman," or,

"Why I shouldn't go to an 'All You Can Eat' diner which only serves beans."

She said her rate was one hundred and fifty dollars an hour! This had better be worth it! I made one hundred and fifty dollars per <u>month</u>, or something like that… when I wasn't selling crack.

She asked, "Vot seems to be your problem young man?"

She crossed her varicose-veined legs which looked like green snakes, wriggling on her calves, trying to escape to attack me. I was reminded of the serpent offering an apple to Adam and Eve. Maybe the serpent had escaped from Eve's legs! That was why Adam fled the Garden of Eden followed by his complaining wife. God! To think he gave up a rib for her! Talk about the short end of the stick…

Dr. Angela cleared her throat to regain my attention. (I had to remember to tell her about my other problem: ADD. Not ADD as with math, but ADD as in Attention Deficit Disorder).

"I don't like girls," I said.

"Do you like boys, zen?"

"No I hate them as much as girls."

"Vy do you hate girls and boys? Do you like sex?"

"Not right now thank you," I said impulsively.

"Zat is not vot I vas asking!" she said as she put her notebook down, removed her spectacles (not designed by Georgio Armani) and glared at me. *This isn't going to work out. The bitch is becoming too aggressive. Maybe I should find another shrink.*

But then I noticed a glossy of a hot chick in a picture frame on her desk, and thought she might introduce me to her sometime, if I paid my bill, which I seldom did these days. Tough times you know, recession and all that. *McDonalds* wasn't hiring anymore and I didn't have the right attitude to be a *Walmart* Greeter. THESE ARE THE WORLD'S LARGEST EMPLOYERS! WHY WON'T THEY HIRE ME? DO THEY KNOW ABOUT MY MENTAL CONDITION? DO THEY CARE? I recall a *Walmart* greeter glaring at me as he suspected I had shoplifted a canoe. Can you believe it? He only glared at me! I hadn't paid for it as I walked out of the store with the canoe over my head.

Anyway, back to the bitch doctor. "OK, OK," I responded, "maybe I like sex. Is that a photo of your daughter?"

She turned around and placed the picture face down on her desk. *Shit! How will I pass the time now? Can't stand gazing at that abstract crap on her wall, and wouldn't dare look up her skirt.*

"Let me rephrase zee question," she said as she turned around, picked up her notebook and stared at me impassively.

"Do you have any sexual desires?" she asked, her pen poised to take questionable notes.

"Can we stop talking about sex?" I asked.

"Zen vot <u>do</u> you vont to talk about? Vy did you come here in zer first place? All my patients talk about sex."

"I'm not a pervert," I said righteously, as the circumstances demanded.

"My other patients are not perverts eezer! Zey come here for help to make zem function in zer real world!"

"How old is your daughter?" I asked.

"Please do not ask questions about my daughter!"

"But you asked me to talk. Whose line is it anyway? I want to talk about your daughter."

"You may not!" She scribbled something in her notebook, ripped out the sheet and gave it to me.

"Vot does that look like?" she asked.

"A prescription for *Viagra*?" I hazarded.

"No, no. What else does it remind you of?"

"A forest?" I answered.

"Ah goot. Zo you like Nature."

"Naturally," I laughed.

She didn't find that funny and no smile came from those thin cruel lips. I wondered if she was Hitler's secret grand-daughter. Maybe she was going to torture me to death. *Vee hav vays to make you talk*...maybe that cute ass receptionist would come in with a pair of pliers to pull out my teeth, toenails and fingernails after she strapped me to the couch.

The fear prompted me to say: "I see many trees. Coniferous, deciduous and voluminous. I see the birds and the bees."

"Enough," she said, taking the sheet back from me "you are not being zerious. If you vont me to help you, zen you must not play games wiz me."

"But I like games, I like to tease people," I said, grabbing the sheet back from her gnarled hands.

"I see tranquility in the forest, I hear birds singing. I am walking alone, at peace with myself. I see my father, that drunken son of a bitch whom I never met."

"Your fazzer?"

"Father," I corrected.

"Is zat vy you harbour such anger? Because you are a bastard?"

"No, I was not angry when I was a little bastard, because all my neighbours were sons of bitches."

"Tell me about your muzzer."

"Mother! Not much to tell. She was always out with the sailors."

"Ver you ever molested in your house by anyvon?" she asked, pencil quivering over her blue notebook which likely harboured many tales of weird patient imaginings. I wanted to ask her why she couldn't pronounce any words with 'th' in them, but since she had a sharp pencil near my loins, I had to be careful.

"Can I ask you to say: Thirty-three thrushes thrashing through the thicket?" I asked curiously.

"You may not," she snapped. "Please answer my question. I am here to help you!"

"No, I was never molested in my youth."

"Vell?"

"When I was sixteen, I was attacked by six females with big bosoms and great legs."

"Goot," she said.

"Why do you say it is goot? I mean, good?" I asked, "It was bad."

She chuckled, "Vell, a teenager being pursued by six sexy females could be a fantasy come true, ja?"

"It could have been. But they were chasing me out of the store."

"But vy? Did you steal somezing?"

"No, I had thought they were mannequins and was, sort of, like, you know, kind-a-thing, you know, feeling the curves…"

"You could not tell zey were <u>not</u> mannequins?"

"Not really, they looked so much like Babette."

"So you have girl friend who looks like a mannequin?"

"Not anymore. She took off."

"Vot happened?"

"Well. It was after the blow job."

"Vot is a blow job?"

"I'll show you sometime," I responded.

"Zank you."

"The pleasure will be all mine." I said coolly.

"So vot happened wiz zee blow job?"

"Well, the Hobby Shop filled the canister with helium, instead of air. So Babette, my blow up doll, flew out of my bathroom window. I wish she would come <u>in</u> through the bathroom window. Like that song by the Beatles."

"*Volkswagen* has a song?" she asked.

"No, the singing group: The Beatles."

"Ah, never heard of zem. But zat must have been quite a sight," she said, "but vee must find you a real substitute. Vy did you tell me that you didn't like girls ven you do?"

"That is my problem Dr. Angela. I only see women as objects. I cannot relate to real women. I like them wet and rubbery like Babette."

"Ze time is up. Come and see me again next week and don't forget to pay on ze way out. How you say 'make wiz ze money'?"

The following week I returned and Miss Cute Ass smiled and said: "Ze doctor vill see you now."

On opening the door, I was surprised to see another woman sitting in the chair. Hair as black and shiny as a raven's feathers, crowned with a black pillbox hat, and a black rubber wetsuit that clung to her curves like paint on my 86 Honda. Wow! I wish I was her painter! Would have really been my pet project. I hesitated. *Who was this new doctor who looked like Babette, my blow up doll?*

"Iz OK. Iz me. I change to suit my patients. Maybe you vill tell me more about yourself now."

Well this doc was hot! Man, really hot! I just couldn't restrain myself and grabbed her by her tight little ass and pulled her onto the couch.

"Jonboy! Vot are you doing? Control yourself! Stop zat, you naughty little boy... Jonboy...don't do zat to me... Jonbooooooy! Ahhhhh..."

We got married the following week and have been happily married since. And you know what? If I ever lose Angela, I have a replacement already in the trunk. Always carry a spare.

You never know what hazards may lurk on the Road of Life...

Lest We Remember

"Was it a shared room?" I asked.

"Yes" she replied.

"Can I speak to him now?" The woman hesitated.

"Is there a problem?" I asked.

"Yes. He may not be able to speak with you."

"Does he understand English?"

"Yes, but..."

"Take me to him please." I followed her to the lounge.

"There by the window. The man with the blue blazer."

She walked away, her crepe soles soundlessly taking her down the long hallway illuminated with a deathly cold light. The man I wanted to see was seated next to a large bay window. The sunlight cast sharp shadows on his creased face as he sat by himself reminiscing, no doubt, about a life that had gone by too quickly. Outside the window there was a blaze of red and blue pansies neatly placed in window boxes on the balcony. His gaze, however, was fixed on three small boys playing soccer in the field across the street.

"Hello sir," I greeted him. He didn't seem to notice. I moved so that he could see me and smiled down at him. "Hello, I'm Eric."

"Derek?" he asked, with a hint of a smile on his lips, grey eyes searching my face. I didn't contradict him.

"Do I know you?" he asked.

"I don't think so."

45

"I don't recognize your uniform. It's not from the Regiment; that I know," he said as he inspected my navy blue uniform.

"No sir, I am not in a Regiment. I am a police officer."

"Police officer eh? Military police?"

"No sir."

He then paused for several minutes as his gaze shifted back to the young boys in the field. They positioned themselves for shooting a goal, while one of them played goal-keeper.

"My grandchildren..." he said with a smile.

"Fine young boys. You should be proud of them." I responded knowing that these were not his grandchildren.

He remained silent as I sat across from him. In the last year I had been called four times to this facility. The first visit had been difficult because it was hard for me to comprehend the action by the person I had questioned at that time. But then, after discussing the matter with others in my department, I was shocked to find that this was not an uncommon occurrence across the country. The person I was visiting now was quite unlike the other four. Although he sat quietly with hands resting on the armrests of a recliner, I could sense that this man was different. Very different. He had a quiet confidence as he sat gazing into the distance at scenes that his mind likely replayed many times. I could sense that if he stood up, it would undoubtedly have been with a rigid posture of a person of some authority.

He gripped my arm firmly and suddenly began to speak, words flowed like a deluge. A flood of memories which he could not contain in this brief moment of lucidity.

"There were hundreds of them. But my buddies and I were dropped off in darkness behind their lines on the cliffs overlooking the sea. It was there that we began our operations that would change the course of the battle we were fighting. Those bloody Krauts. I got rid of twenty of them before I got back to my buddies."

In between spasms of coughing, he continued to describe in graphic detail how, under the black night sky in a place called Anzio, Italy, he had killed the enemy with his bare hands, as they tried to hold onto their key positions. The torrent of vivid recollections poured out unabated while his brow furrowed and his eyes glinted with the fierceness of that of a warrior.

46

It was hard to believe that these words were coming from this gentle old man reliving an event which had occurred many decades ago. His back straightened as he spoke, his eyes peered angrily from their sunken sockets, and his fingers bent like the talons of a falcon ready to catch its prey. The transformation was startling, but his memories had suffused his body with strength from his past. The aggressive actions, many decades before, were rekindling the vigour of youth in this old man.

He started to cough again and the words ceased. The old soldier looked outside the window again and then looked at me. "Where is Madeleine?"

"Madeleine?" I asked.

"Why didn't you bring your mother?"

"I'm sorry sir, I ..."

"Why won't she visit me? They told me she would be coming."

He looked away this time, his gaze shifted to the pansies and his head bowed down to the floor as his shoulders shook with violent sobs.

"Perhaps she will be," I said, rising to leave and touching his shoulder gently.

I was taken to his room which was now being cleaned with that strong-smelling disinfectant commonly used in these places. On the wall, a brown and white photograph of a handsome young man in uniform gazed back at me. A bronze star, embossed with an 'R' in the centre, hung from the wall at the end of a red, white and green ribbon. On a small chest by his bed was the portrait of a dark haired woman standing next to a rock by the seaside. This was likely the 'Madeleine' he had spoken of. There were no more recent pictures on the table or in the drawers of the chest.

Back at the station I searched for information relating to Joseph Johnson but, other than driving through a Stop sign more than twenty years ago, there was no other information. Instead I looked at similar incidents. There had been five cases of this type across Canada this year that had been classified as homicides. Annually, several hundred confrontations had been reported, with some injuries, but no charges had ever been laid.

I left the Glengarry Nursing Home and went to the morgue to look at the body. The victim was an old grizzled man likely in his eighties. There had been a severe blow to the back of his head, and there was one large indentation on his skull, which had likely resulted in his immediate death. I closed the door of the morgue and went back to the station to begin my report. After completing details related to the name, address of assailant, and victim, I hesitated when I came to the section on *"Charges"*.

I thought again of what I had seen of the assailant. An old man, locked in his memories of six decades ago, reliving the exuberance and tragedies of his youthful days on the sun-splashed beaches of Italy, whose white sands and turquoise waters had been reddened by the blood of his comrades and his enemies. The training he had received as a young soldier in the Special Forces had been rigorous, punishing and brutal, but nonetheless necessary in those dark days of the 1940's. Regrettably, that training had been so deeply ingrained in him, that his long life had failed to diminish the aggression that was now part of his being.

The Form L1032, line 15, asked:

Proceed with Charges?

I entered: 'No.'

Reason for not proceeding with Charges?

I hesitated, and then typed: 'Act was performed by a person with diminished capacity who was unaware of his actions.'

The case was closed.

The Bargain Hunter

The young girl looked outside the window of her temporary home and tried to focus her eyes. A blanket of white stretched towards the horizon, hiding any distinguishing features of the landscape. The view was in sharp contrast to her native province of Hainan, where a turquoise ocean also stretched far into the distance. Snow, blown by high winds the previous evening, had created a snowdrift which almost reached the bottom of the windowsill. But she had gladly accepted the job in this remote location because it was a fulfillment of her childhood dream. As she continued to gaze in awe at this silent, snowy landscape, she heard a motorized vehicle approaching, hurling clouds of snow in its wake.

"Are you expecting anyone this morning sir?" she asked.

"No I'm not. Why do you ask?" The old man shifted uneasily on the sofa by the fireplace. He had just thrown another log on the fire. It crackled before bursting into flame, suffusing the cozy cottage with the scent of pine.

"Someone is coming here very fast sir," she replied as she squinted through the frosted glass at the approaching intruder.

The old man slowly got to his feet and adjusted his coat over his bulky midriff. "Close the curtains and sound the alarm for the workshop. The boys need to know of our uninvited visitor. They will know what to do." The young girl quickly pulled the curtain and locked the door.

"I'll stand here and you peek through the peephole and tell me what you see," he said, as he shuffled into a corner nearest to the entrance. The machine stopped a few feet from the door.

"It looks like a motorcycle rickshaw on skis."

"It's a snowmobile," whispered the old man. "Remember Miss Le Tow, we are not in your homeland. No rickshaws here, you know."

"A person is getting out now and coming to the door. He's wearing a blue uniform and there is the letter 'W' on his coat."

"Are you sure it's the letter 'W'?" the old man whispered.

Miss Le Tow nodded. There was a knock on the door. "Should I open the door sir?" asked the girl. The old man shook his head.

"But it's cold outside and maybe he will get sick, sir."

"He won't get sick. Ignore him and he'll go away. I know who he is. He is the last person I want in our place. How did he find us?"

"Nowadays they have GPS, sir," said Miss Le Tow.

"GPS? What's that?"

"It helps someone to navigate to any destination on the globe sir," she whispered, pleased that she could show the old man that she knew something he didn't.

"But our address is not listed, so how did he find us?"

"Everyone knows you sir. If they want to find you they will. But who is he?"

"Well, I know his type and the company he keeps. That's all I need to know."

"But it's minus thirty outside now, and he must be very cold sir," she implored, unaccustomed to seeing anyone standing in the cold for so long.

"Look Miss Le Tow. You're new here so you may not know this man. But I think I know who he is. If he wants warmth, he can go to China instead."

"China? What would he do in China sir?"

"Well, you are still learning the ropes aren't you little Miss Le Tow? They have bargain prices in your homeland and that's where these guys go all the time. They take advantage of your poor countrymen who work long hours for very little money."

"Oh, but it's so cold outside sir and there has been so much snow. And it's all white."

"All right you said?"

"No sir, I said all <u>white</u>. It was snowing heavily and is very cold."

"But people of your age, you know, the snow, it's a little of what you fancy isn't it?"

"Yes sir, I do fancy it. But he is not dressed properly although he is dressed in style, with a light blue suit and a light blue overcoat. But the coat doesn't look very warm. He must not have known it would be cold when he was putting it on before coming out."

"Pudding? Did he bring pudding?"

"No sir. I said <u>putting</u>, not pudding. Putting it on. His light overcoat with the 'W' on it. Oh, I'm sorry you can't hear me very well because you have your hat pulled over your ears."

"Ha! It's probably his company's uniform for the season. Is he still there?"

"Yes sir but it looks like he is going. He just started his snow-rickshaw. But why wouldn't you open the door for him? It is after all the season to be nice." The old man grunted but did not reply.

Miss Le Tow watched as the man and his snowmobile disappeared over the distant snow banks. She was very curious as to why her boss didn't open the door since he was known to be such a loveable person. She couldn't help but feel privileged to begin work here after she had put in her application earlier in the month. Being brought to this location was a treat for her. She had never been airborne before and found the trip to be magical.

Her curiosity prompted her to ask: "You are such a kind man sir, but why didn't you let that man in?"

The old man laughed as he settled back into his couch by the fire, lit his pipe and took a few puffs. "He was a Bargain Hunter looking for deals from Suppliers. These guys can't fool me. There is no way that we are going to give him anything! He was a Buyer from one of the big stores who goes all over the world looking for bargains. Perhaps he had to pay more in China, and that is why he has come here hoping he could get lots of free stuff. And one more thing, Miss Le Tow. Don't keep calling me 'sir'."

Now Miss Le Tow understood, even though she was only six years old. "Thanks Santa," she said. "I'll go to the workshop now and tell the elves the man from *Walmart* has gone."

"Ho! Ho! Ho! Soon it will be time to go," said Santa, as he settled down by the fireplace to rest up before the busy night ahead.

Until Debt Do Us Part

Robert E. Billings felt secure in this mountain retreat but things had been changing and he was getting a little bit worried. It had all started on Halloween when the phone rang at midnight. A male voice had asked: "May I speak to Robert E. Billings?" And then there was a loud bang, as if someone had slammed a car door. Then the call ended. Just like that. At the time he thought it was a Halloween prank and went back to sleep. Some days later the phone rang again, but there was only silence on the other end. A dead silence.

It was now mid-November and he was sipping an after dinner wine in *The Grizzly Bar*, his favourite restaurant in Banff.

"Another glass of wine?" the waiter asked.

"No thanks, I'm fine. Should be leaving now, it's getting late," he said as he fished out his wallet. The waiter removed the plate and cutlery from his table.

"Merlot. I like that too. After I graduated from Baby Duck," the young man laughed.

"Carol is off tonight. Is she?" asked Billings giving him his *MasterCard*.

"She has a new dog. Trying to train it."

"Never owned one myself, but she does seem to be a dog person," smiled Billings. "You new in town?"

"Yes sir, moonlighting at the moment so I can pay for my studies. Good Arts school here in Banff."

"Brian!" The bartender called. "New customers at the door!"

"Sorry sir, be back in a moment."

Billings looked at his watch and noted that it was too late for his regular walk on the bank of the Bow River. Brian returned with the credit card.

"You've been in town long, Mr. Billings?" he asked.

"This year will make twenty years, young man," he said, as he put on his overcoat.

"See you again Mr. Billings. Have a good evening!"

Billings ambled out of *The Grizzly Bar*. It was a quiet restaurant, unlike the others which were frequented by rambunctious skiers and outdoors types. He had been coming here at least twice a week for the last few months. He liked Carol, the waitress who had started work there about six weeks ago. She was quite chatty with him and he looked forward to seeing her. He guessed she was just turning twenty. Billings would be hitting fifty soon. Then he'd be a dirty old man…for yearning the company of someone so young.

A week later Billings was back at *The Grizzly Bar*. Carol was not there but Brian smiled and came over.

"Nice to see you again Mr. Billings." He pulled a chair for Billings to get seated. "Do you live close by?"

"Not too close. A little place just on the outskirts of town, near the river." Billings removed his coat and placed it on the chair back and sat down.

"Oh, so it <u>was</u> you walking by the river day before yesterday. I noticed you were limping. Did you sprain your ankle during your walk?"

"No, no. Nothing like that. Just an accident, many years ago. My leg bothers me when it gets cold, or when I'm tired, or stressed."

"Serious one?" Brian asked as he poured Billings his glass of Merlot. Billings hesitated. He preferred not to discuss the accident but the young man seemed sympathetic and genuine.

"Just a minor collision."

"And?" asked Brian politely.

"Just hurt my leg," said Billings as Brian over-poured the wine, apologized profusely and placed a napkin on the wet tablecloth.

"Sorry about that Mr. Billings. I was just distracted. Too much homework."

"No problem," said Billings. "You shouldn't work so hard. Especially in this happy town."

Nice young man thought Billings. *Face seems familiar.* He ate his food, paid the bill, and said goodbye to Brian. Outside, he inhaled the juniper scented air deeply. He loved living in the mountains where the air was always fresh and scented and where people were not always in a hurry. The lamplight was slightly dimmed by light flakes of snow as he trudged half a block to his Toyota. There was something on his windshield. It was a small envelope. *Probably an invitation to a new restaurant* he thought.

Billings put the envelope into his pocket and got into his car. After arriving home, he removed his shoes, hung up his overcoat in the hallway closet and went to his den where he found the remote and turned on his TV. He felt his shirt pocket to look for his glasses. He needed these to read the newspaper during the commercials but pulled out the envelope instead. His glasses were on the coffee table and he put them on. The handwritten noted was addressed to him: *Robert E. Billings. Confidential.*

Must be a new personalized way to hand out parking tickets, he smiled. Inside the envelope was a folded piece of lined paper with a note: "*You have a debt. It must be paid. Soon.*" He crumpled the paper and threw it into the wastebasket. *Must be the wrong Billings, or some stupid joke.*

Something was gnawing his gut. Robert E. Billings's pulse rate quickened as he pulled the note out of the wastebasket and looked at it again. "*You have a debt. It must be paid. Soon.*"

Could this really be a joke? No. Too sinister for a practical joke. He had no enemies among his neighbours, or at Hellman's Insurance Agency where he worked. There were only six persons in the office and they all got along quite well. No nasty politics or back stabbing like in his previous job. What had he done recently to provoke someone? Maybe it was that door-to-door salesman selling a new Electricity contract which he had declined. Perhaps too rudely. No, not likely. Maybe it was that Halloween Caller again. "Odd, very odd," he said softly, "Has to be a mistake."

It was a long night for Robert E Billings. Sleep did not come to him easily as he twisted from side to side, a worm of fear burrowing in his brain. Finally, he dozed off.

He awoke the next morning when the neighbour's dog Brutus was barking. A dog could never be his best friend. He had a deep seated fear of dogs, small, medium or large. They never liked him and always growled when he approached. They likely smelled his fear from a block away.

He opened the door to retrieve the newspaper and unfolded it on his dining room table. Billings prepared his usual breakfast of two eggs, bacon and two pieces of toast and sat at the table. Out of the corner of his eye the waste paper basket seemed to be beckoning. He took a sip of coffee to moisten his dry throat, went to the wastebasket and pulled out the note. He cleaned his reading glasses with a paper napkin just to make sure that he had not misread the message the previous night. *'You have a debt…'* he threw it back into the basket. *Rotten joke, you son of a bitch, whoever you are!*

The following Saturday he needed to get some groceries: bread, some sausages, eggs, Kraft Dinners for the quick meal or snack. He opened his car door, put the key in the ignition and noticed an audiotape protruding from his tape deck. He never listened to audio tapes in his car. Someone must have put this one in! He pulled it out. There was a green and white label on the generic cassette tape. It said: *'Listen to me Robert E. Billings.'*

Billings sat down in the driver's seat and looked left, right and behind him. White knuckles gripped the steering wheel. His frenzied brain told him to fling the tape out of the window, or to throw it into the nearest garbage can. *I am not a scared rabbit!* He shouted silently to himself. His unsteady fingers finally pushed the tape into the deck. There was a soft rumble as the tape made its first few revolutions. Then a click and then a low voice, so low that he moved his head forward to listen to the speaker in his dash. *"Enjoy your day Mr. Billings."* A pause, another click, and then, *"It will be your last one."*

The eggs and bacon he had for breakfast reversed up his gullet. Billings was getting scared. Very, very, scared. He had not felt this way since he was a little boy, when he almost walked into a Doberman that had just turned the corner. *I'm being so stupid. This must be a joke! 'Enjoy your day Billings. It will be your last one,'* echoed in his mind while his fingers trembled. The voice bounced off the walls of his skull seeming to gain volume until he closed his eyes and mouthed: *Stop!* Robert E. Billings was angry. Very, very, angry. He would take care of this joker, whoever he was.

The Toyota's engine purred as he made a left turn onto Moose Avenue and continued on until he came to the Safeway store where he picked up what he needed and returned home. He slowly opened the door, peered behind it and then stepped inside. He checked the closets, behind the sofa and under his bed. The day moved slowly with Billings looking out the window for strangers, checking to make sure all the doors and windows were shut. *I'm getting paranoid!*

He needed to go for his usual walk by the Bow River and maybe get a hold of himself. It was always a nice place to walk when it was close to sunset. It may quiet his churning gut. Just as Billings was leaving the town limits, he noticed a woman walking on the side of the road, going in the same direction as he was. *Should pick her up, get my mind of my problems*, he thought. He slowed down and recognized the woman. It was Carol, from the restaurant. *What a relief!*

"Need a ride somewhere?" he asked cheerily.

"Mr. Billings! What a surprise! No, I don't need a ride but you can help me. My dog just took off into the trees by the river. Maybe you can help me find her." *A dog! Oh God! I must control myself! As long as she's with me it shouldn't be a problem. Anyway, maybe it will be a poodle. Less scary. She seems to be a poodle lover.*

"Sure thing!" said Robert E Billings nervously, always ready to help a damsel in distress, especially one as cheerful and attractive as young Carol. He pulled the car onto the shoulder and got out, pleased with this welcome distraction.

"She might be among the trees. I'll go back a hundred feet or so and you continue on, along the river. I'll catch up with you. Yell, if you see her Mr. Billings."

"Will do," said Billings as he pushed through the dense brush bordering the slope to the river. Carol was already down the slope and had turned right along the bank and was thirty paces away.

"Her name is Xena. A Husky cross!" she called out. Billings hesitated. *A Husky Cross! Shit! That's a big dog, maybe I should tell her that I'm not feeling well and need to go home. No, no. I need her company.*

Billings looked left along the river bank and worked his way carefully over the slippery stones. It was 5.30 p.m. and the sun would be setting soon. He turned and saw that Carol had stopped and was now coming in his direction much to his relief. Still no sign of her dog. It was perceptibly cooler and a slight fog had risen above the water. Up ahead he could see someone. The person had a dog on a leash. *Great! That must be her dog…glad someone is holding her.*

Carol was now coming closer after also having seen the figure of the man and the dog ahead. "That looks like Xena!" she shouted.

The dog and the man now approached them. As they drew closer he recognized Brian, the waiter from the restaurant, leading Xena by a stout leash.

"Hey there Brian! You found him!" he shouted happily, but kept a safe distance from the animal.

The dog began to growl, and as it drew closer, ahead of Brian, he noticed its ice blue eyes staring at him intently. The growl became deeper. Billings stepped backwards and could almost hear his knees knocking. *This is a scary beast! Not very friendly at all.*

"Hello Mr. Billings. Xena! Sit!" The dog obeyed. Brian held the leash tightly while he waited for Carol. Billings dared not take his eyes off Xena. He quickly looked over his shoulder to explore the fastest path up towards the road if he needed to escape, should Xena pull the leash out of Brian's hand.

"Gotta get back to the restaurant. Keep the leash around your wrist." Brian handed the leash to Carol.

Xena stood up and growled again, opening her mouth wider to show many incisors, saliva dripping from her jaws. Billing's leg started to throb. He doubted he could run if he had to.

"Want to walk with us Mr. Billings?" asked Carol. Noting his hesitation, she raised her hand to Xena.

"Don't look into her eyes. She may think you're challenging her."

"She would be mistaken; I can assure you." Billings laughed nervously. "Challenging a sixty-pound dog would be the farthest thing from my mind."

He fell in step with Carol as she walked slowly along the bank, shielding Billings from Xena's malevolent eyes. The river snaked into the distance, whitecaps shimmering in the dying light of the sunset. A gray cloud swallowed the last rays of the setting sun.

"Xena was an abused dog. I rescued her last month from a very nasty man here in Banff. He had her tied up to a tree with a chain all day and night, while he drank himself stupid. I would walk by and throw her some food.

She took to me, and never growled or barked at me, like she did to others. One day I entered his yard and she came to me and licked my hand. I knew then that I had a friend."

"And a protector," offered Billings.

"Yes, a protector. The man told me to take her and just asked me for a case of *Labatts* as payment. That may be the only time in my life when alcohol actually bought me security."

"Oh? You were a heavy drinker?"

"No. I was an orphan Mr. Billings. Since I was a year old."

"You were adopted?"

"I wasn't born in Banff. I came here looking for someone. I think I found him."

"You mean Brian?" Carol looked behind her shoulder. Brian could still be seen walking on the river bank in the distance.

"I found Brian two years ago... through Facebook."

"A long distance romance?"

"It wasn't a romance, Mr. Billings. He was searching too, and he believes he too, has found what he was also looking for."

"Not a romance then?"

"No. He's my twin brother."

"Aha, no wonder I noticed a resemblance when I first met him!"

"He was in a foster home, just like me. But a different one. As bad as the one I was in for fifteen years of my life, until I ran away and came here. My foster parents were alcoholics. Serious alcoholics who loved to discipline me, with relish, countless times a day. Then they got into drugs. Money for drugs, but not for groceries. That's when I had had enough and ran away."

"How terrible! Didn't Social Services check up on them?"

"I'm sure they did, in the first few years. After that they assumed they had the right home for me. They did make sure that I was sent to school. School was heaven for me. Away from my abusers."

58

"How sad."

"Very sad Mr. Billings. But Brian had a much more difficult time."

"How's that?"

"In his foster home the father was a Scout Leader."

"So he learned about the outdoors then?"

"No. He learned about the <u>back</u> door, if you'll excuse the crude analogy. The man was a pedophile. His wife may not have known it. Brian was too scared to tell anyone. He escaped when he was fourteen. Lived on the street most of the time until he found *The Crossroads Shelter* for homeless teens in Toronto. They treated him well and got him on his feet again."

"So you are from Toronto then?"

Carol stopped, reached into her pocket and took out a silver wrapper, unfolded it and popped a *Juicy Fruit* gum into her mouth. The rising moon shed its silver light on Xena's grey and white fur.

"Just like you Mr. Billings. You also lived in Toronto." Her words came slowly, deliberately. He could sense that it was perhaps accusatory.

There was a rustling in the tree above. Xena looked up. A night owl hooted briefly and flew away sensing imminent danger below.

"I don't remember telling you that."

"You didn't, Mr. Billings. My biological parents were killed in an accident. Twenty years ago. In Toronto." Carol's jaws worked harder as she chewed on her gum. She loosened her grip on Xena's leash and stopped walking.

"I wanted to know what happened. I did an investigation of my own." Carol continued chewing on her gum. Her eyes, narrow slits in the dim light, glared at Billings. "After finding out who my parents were, I read old newspaper reports and also got the Police notes through the Freedom of Information Act. <u>You</u> were driving the other car Mr. Billings! It appears there were no witnesses at the time of impact. The officer at the scene smelled alcohol in your car and suspected you drove through the red light. You survived because there was an airbag on the driver's side but the one on the passenger's side was not functional. Your wife was killed, along with my parents. But you survived! However, the officer said you were unconscious behind the airbag."

She paused. Billings's leg continued to throb with growing intensity. He wanted to run but his leg hurt too much.

"Or you seemed to be. You were faking it, weren't you Mr. Billings? The officer couldn't take a Breathalyzer test and, to your good fortune, the hospital forgot to take a blood sample since they were trying to revive you. You kept faking it! You didn't even care about your wife! No charges were laid due to lack of evidence. You moved here to be forgotten. And to forget. Didn't you Mr. Billings?" Her voice became a gunshot when she mentioned his name.

Billings looked left and right, hoping to narrow down a fast escape route. He felt that Xena could smell his blood which his heart was pumping at a furious pace through his swollen veins.

"It took three years to find you. You killed my parents didn't you Mr. Billings?" The leash fell from Carol's hand.

"No, no! I didn't do it!" Billings backed away.

Xena took a step closer, jaws partially open to bare her white fangs. Her ears were flat, pointed backwards and her tail was raised. She crouched, and a deep growl, like that of a demon from Hades, emanated from her throat. The moonlight caught flecks of perspiration on his forehead which Xena would soon savour.

"Xena can tell you are lying. You killed my parents! And your wife! You stole our childhood. Five lives destroyed, Mr. Billings. By your drunkenness. You must pay!"

Billing's lungs laboured to suck in air. Much needed air. He tried to flee. His legs, heavy as if shackled by leg irons, stepped backwards as Xena advanced slowly, ready to pounce, silhouette large against the rising moon. *I can make it,* he thought. Foolishly. He should have known that you never turn your back and run from a predator. But Robert E. Billings clambered up the slope, fingers grabbing shrubs, roots, grass, anything to escape the Husky-Wolf hybrid. Carol watched, hands in her pockets, her gum more flavourful as he stumbled down the bank. With fierce snarls, Xena pounced on her fleeing prey and gripped his larynx. Her fangs ruptured his windpipe. Wild, vicious blue-white eyes glared into his, while his lungs screamed for air. Billings's fingers clung to Xena's neck trying to push away her large jaws, voracious for his blood. His last vision was of bloodshot, blue-white eyes staring into his, as the creature's large head swung his own back and forth. His last smell was that of foul dog breath puffing into his bleeding nostrils. His head moved slower and slower like a large pendulum counting down the end of the life of Robert E. Billings. Xena dragged her kill back to her mistress. Carol spat her gum like a wad of chewing tobacco on the bloodied corpse.

She pulled the body down the slope and kicked it into the iridescent waters. A wake of black water followed the dead man as his body was pulled into the faster moving current toward the river bend. Xena sat on her haunches and howled. The call reverberated off the stark mountain face. First one, then two, and then a pack of her distant cousins joined in the celebration of the full moon. Carol dropped to her knees and put her arms around Xena's warm shoulders. Together they watched as the corpse of Robert E. Billings was swallowed up in the darkening waters.

The debt was paid. In full.

The First Time

"No let's not do it."

"Why not?"

"I'm not ready yet."

"But why? Are you afraid?"

"Yes, and I don't want my mum to find out. She thinks the world of me. Besides, I'm only seventeen. She wants me to go to university. I don't want anything to happen to me."

"University is shit. Look, we've been together for what? One year now? And you still don't want to do it? My first time was when I was fourteen. Can you believe that? Fourteen years old! I hadn't started to shave yet but I didn't fuckin' care…"

"Oh Jimmy. You know I love you. But I just don't want to do it. Guys are different. Guys can do these things but I can't."

"We've talked about this before and you said it may be OK. So why don't you want to do it?"

"Because… I dunno, like I said. I don't feel good about it. It's not right. We don't need to do this tonight."

"Are you getting religious on me or something?"

"No Jimmy. You know I've never been religious."

"So what's with you?"

"It's dark and creepy out here, and look! There's a police car ahead."

"It's white but it's not a police car. I'm sure of it. We'll walk by close to it and I'll check. But let me do it. Don't let them look at you. Look the other way when we pass it, OK? And don't panic."

"OK."

"It's not a police car and there was no one in it."

"Oh Jimmy, let's go back to where there's more light. I'm getting scared. I'm not ready for this."

"Now look. There are some trees and bushes ahead. That's where we'll go. No one can see us in there. As long as you're real quiet. Can you be quiet for a few minutes?"

"No, it's too creepy. I think I'm going to be sick."

"Relax. Take a deep breath. Are you afraid you may get hurt?"

"No. It's not that. It's just…"

"Just what?"

"We shouldn't be doing this. Look! There are two guys coming our way."

"Just ignore them. OK?"

"They are pretty big guys. Maybe they're cops."

"They are not cops. Cops walk differently. These guys are just losers. Maybe a couple of drunks. Ignore them. Look straight ahead."

"One of them looked at us."

"No. they looked at you. Just horny drunks. Didn't you smell the booze?"

"Yeah. You're probably right. I'm still scared. I want to go home."

"It's your first time. After that you'll be fine."

"Oh Jimmy. I don't know. I just don't feel good about this. Can we please go home?"

"No. We have to do this tonight. Otherwise you'll never want to. Its dark among the trees and no one can see us."

"Someone is bound to see us and then we'll really be in trouble. I'm so young. I don't want to do this."

"No one will see us. Take off your coat."

"Can't we wait until tomorrow?"

"You see that guy coming our way?"

"He looks scary. He's big. He's seen us. He's coming right towards us Jimmy."

"Just be very quiet. He can't see us."

"I'm scared."

"Be quiet. He may hear us."

"Ok."

"Ohhhh."

"Ssshh."

"No. Stop. Don't hurt me."

"I won't hurt you but do what I say."

"Aaahhhhh…"

"Stop it Jimmy! Stop it! Stop now!"

"Can't! Gotta finish the job."

"What have you done?!"

"Be quiet. Someone will hear us."

"But there's so much blood. Someone will find out what we've done here."

"Don't worry. Shit! What the fuck?"

"What Jimmy?"

"Fuck, Fuck, Fuck! Asshole!"

"I'm going to be sick Jimmy."

"It's like that sometimes."

"But look what you did. I'm going to throw up."

"This is your first time. Maybe the next guy will have more money. To think I killed this asshole for only five bucks…"

The Hit Man

Carlito carefully covered his left ear with a lock of greased black hair. He had lost a piece of his ear in a fight when he was a teenager. But he had won that fight and had given that son of a bitch something he would never forget. A kick in the nuts to make sure that he would never father any offspring. But that was many fights and many years ago. He was now a man. Working for Don Vito himself. He was proud of what Don Vito had said in the meeting with the boys that morning.

"He didda good job. Kept the Sicilian honour. Here, takea this gift from me. Share it witta your mama." He gave Carlito a leather briefcase which likely held a few thousand dollars as a bonus. The Don was a generous man.

"You know watta our Carlito did?" Don Vito turned to the others. "You know that big Colombian guy who come into our territory? Well, he's gone now." Don Vito chuckled. "He gotta bullet hole in each eye and spaghetti and meatballs stuffed in his mouth. Carlito then putta him on his chair at his dining room table. You mess with Don Vito, and Carlito will takea care of you."

Don Vito rose from his leather chair and gave Carlito a kiss on both cheeks. He handed Carlito's cell phone to the others which showed a picture of the Colombian having a posthumous dinner.

Carlito was home now, dressed in a white shirt and black trousers. His mama had washed, dried and pressed his clothes as she always did. Now he was waiting for mama to call him for supper. All good Italian sons stayed with their mamas even after they got married. Carlito wasn't married yet since he was still being groomed by the Don for bigger jobs.

"Don' getta hitched just yet. There's lotsa work to be done. Afta that your mama will find you a good girl and I, Don Vito, will pay for da biggest weddin' you ever seen."

Carlito's father had worked for the Don too, but was killed during a turf war with the Turks when Carlito was only ten years old. The Don had been like a father to him since then. Carlito loved the Don like he had loved his father.

He entered the kitchen and kissed his mama on both cheeks. The smell of garlic laced meatballs made his stomach murmur with anticipation.

"Carlito, sonny boy. Can you do somma ting for your mama?"

"Just tell me mama. You donna have to ask me," he replied.

So she told him. He frowned. It was a difficult job, which he couldn't refuse…it was his mama who was asking him. He wished she had asked someone else. But then the neighbour should not give trouble to his mama. So he, Carlito, would take care of the business. Bruno barked excitedly expecting that Carlito would take him for a walk.

"No Bruno. You must astay inside. Is all your fault. You makea troubles for mama and the neighbour widda your barking and messing around. Now I gotta takea care of it. Do the dirty work."

He put on his gloves to make sure there would be no residue on his hands. He had enough experience in the business to know that one should always be protected. And protection is something he knew a lot about. In his pocket he had his favourite toy which his father had given him for his birthday. His papa, who was so good with a gun, had taught him how to target shoot when he was only four years old. His papa knew a lot about the business. Probably knew that Carlito would get into the same line of work. Too bad he wasn't around to see how great he was with his father's profession, and how much the Don admired his work.

Through a gap in the curtained window, Carlito could see the neighbour sitting on his couch watching television, with the volume on high. He knew that the neighbour was quite deaf but he did not want to take any chances. This was not going to be an easy job. Not in broad daylight. He waited until he was certain that no other neighbours were in their yards, or on the street. Then he made his move, carefully working his way across the yard, looking right and left to make sure he was not missing anything. Years of practice had taught him that a fluttering window curtain, a slight creaking, or a crow cawing was a warning that someone was watching. Someone who would snitch on him. He hated snitches and took care of them when the time came.

He walked across the yard silently, stooping when he needed to. The tree branches hung low close to the neighbour's fence. There was a rustle of leaves over the fence but it was only a cat. A black cat. Definitely a bad sign. He was getting overcautious. He continued around the house, breathing softly, and walking silently. He moved quickly and skillfully towards the neighbour's fence, made sure again that no one was watching, and soon the job was done. The neighbour never had a clue. That's how good Carlito was. He put the remains in a garbage bag and hid it behind a bush. He would dispose of it early in the morning. No one had seen or heard him. He was sure of that.

Carlito opened the kitchen door and nodded to his mama. But her sensitive nose picked up a smell like death when he entered. She held her face in her hands and shouted:

"Sonny. What you gone an' done? Just looka what's on your Guccis!"

"Oh no mama. I done it again. Please mama, I don' wanna pick up dog shit no more."

"Bambino, come to mama." She hugged and kissed him. "We have special dinner tonight. Just for you. But first let me take off your stinky shoes."

Now and then even a Hit Man misses a step and gets into deep shit.

The Mythfit

Once upon a time in BC (no, not British Columbia but before baby Jesus was born) lived a young boy who was a math wizard. He was shy and introverted. Had computers been invented in BC, he would have looked like a computer geek, except that he didn't wear glasses, which hadn't been invented yet either. As a young boy he had been recognized as a genius. His only toys were Lego and Plato-dough. His only friend was Achilles who was known to be well heeled, and he had a horrid neighbour called Herod.

But Harristotal loved numbers. He especially liked playing with his abacus which his father, Scrotumus, had given him for his tenth birthday. Scrotumus was the inventor of the wrist hour glass which was not a very successful invention and was a bit ahead of its time (like two thousand years). However, he had not compromised on the education of his young son. He had sent him to the finest schools in Athens. He was rewarded when he noticed his son taking such an interest in mechanical things, and was especially pleased to see that he spent so much time with his abacus.

The abacus was a much sought after device and was now being perfected in Greece to be capable of greater calculating speeds. It was thought that the Grecian rails on the main frame provided it with that blinding speed. (Later, Grecian Formula provided the slickest wheels in Chariot Racing until the Romans came along with their Alpha Romano). Every two years the speed would double due to the highly developed material being used for the wires, the balls and the frame. Merchants from Europe, Asia and Africa came to trade textiles, spices and hardware in exchange for all the new items being produced by this great country. (Had someone discovered North America at that time, they would have come too, but at that time North America kept a low profile and avoided discovery.)

Harristotal grew up to be a fine young man and followed in his father's proud footsteps. He made the world's first Alpha hourglass, which was the most precise model of that day (many centuries later it morphed into the Omega). This invention was followed by many others, but it was in the year 1 BC that he made a discovery that shook the world of commerce. HarrisTotal discovered a major error had been made by the early builders of the abacus. He hypothesized that the abaci would be unable to do any calculations after the year 1 BC because the abacus lacked two vital balls. Lacking two vital balls is always a severe handicap, even for the highly sophisticated abaci. HarrisTotal himself lacked one ball and was unable to procreate twins, much to his wife's dismay who really wanted to have twins like Castor and Pollux, whom she intended to name Beta and Bollocks.

He stated that the reason why early builders had not used the extra two balls was that these would compromise the speed of these great calculators. But they did not realize what would happen in the new millennium during the year zero. HarrisTotal theorized that due to this significant oversight by the early builders, the world of commerce would grind to a halt and possibly be shut down permanently since this device was used in every aspect of business. The lack of sophistication in the old abaci, which were now so prevalent in the civilized world, would destroy the economies of the countries using these. Businesses large and small would all be affected since their employees, mostly males, would be looking for their missing balls. (At that time women were not allowed to work. They could only lie around in diaphanous gowns drinking wine and eating grapes from silver trays, waiting to entertain men after their hard day of labour). They would ask silly questions like:

"What is green, looks like a snake and follows a rainbow?"

Only the likes of Harristotal knew the answer: 'Liam the lascivious Leprechaun from Limerick, leaping legions to latch onto the snaky, but loosely named, Medusa.'

He theorized further that the impact on the civilized world would be that no more food would be harvested, and no more wood collected for cooking and home heating. The water wells would dry up, ships could not sail, the bullock carts would grind to a halt, and most of the human race would be in a state of chaos leading to civil wars (at that time World Wars did not exist because Germany was not there to start these). *Maybe vee vill vin de next one, ja?*

The Minus Two Ball hypothesis was then dubbed the "M2B Uncertainty." Harristotal published his works on many stone tablets (it was said that he left no stone unturned in his obsession to educate the merchants of the day). He was asked to advise many trading companies on how they should prepare for the new millennium. He was in such great demand that he had to hire several hundred "Ball Boys" to produce more balls for the thousands of abaci (child labour was encouraged in those days similar to modern times in Canada, where young people lug huge bags of newspapers to people's homes in the early morning, in sub-zero conditions).

There was another flurry of activity after Emperor Nero the Zero (who also was the Acting Emperor of Greece) decreed that all traders using the abacus without the two balls must hire consultants to prevent any calamities from happening. He also feared that several arrows could be released unintentionally from the armory and strike him dead should he fiddle while Athens (and Rome) burned.

The word was spreading fast through the civilized world. People were panicking. They were drawing large amounts of water from the wells, stocking up on Greek Salad and Grecian Formula and sharpening their swords (to battle Ball Robbers). Some began the long trek back to the mountain caves in the event there was to be a great calamity. Since there was only one large mountain nearby, Mount Olympus, they had to race to get to the top. (This is believed to be the true beginning of the Olympics, and some runners had to take performance enhancing drugs to keep up with the pack).

HarrisTotal and his crew could not keep up with the demand for their services. They had to manufacture extra strong boxes to hold all the gold they were making with their valuable services. On a parallel path, a new type of service was born: 'The Legal Profession'. Hundreds of new lawyers were urging clients to prepare to sue anything that moved, or didn't move, in the year Zero. (That Sue U 2 virus is still with us today, two thousand years later).

Doomsday was approaching and soon it was New Year's Eve. The M2B virus was about to strike. There were no fireworks in the town square. All the Village People (Macho Macho Men) gathered in the town square and waited for the bell toller to ring those fateful chimes heralding the new millennium. Grim faced they watched, wringing their hands as the darkness began to envelope their dear motherland (or was it fatherland?). The bell toller started the first chime for midnight and then the second, but the villagers panicked and all retreated trembling to their humble homes, ready for the great calamity. The final toll was sounded and after that not a sound was heard, not a creature was stirring, not even a mouse. (Remember that Christmas was not yet a statutory holiday since it was still BC). In fear and trembling the villagers waited in their homes and finally fell asleep not knowing what they would wake up to.

The next morning, they started up their abaci, with the missing balls, and everything seemed to be working! They rebooted ("re-sandled" in those days) their abaci just to be certain, with the same result. The Village People screamed and shouted and stormed the home of HarrisTotal but he and his crew were nowhere to be seen. Their whereabouts were never determined. Theories that he and his group restarted the Mother of all organizations, called the "Ma Fer Ya" in neighbouring Sicily, were never proven. (Nobody ever returned from an investigative visit to Sicily). The M2B theory was confirmed to be a hoax.

The moral of the story is: 'You can fool some of the people some of the time, but you can fool everyone once in a millennium.'

(The above is dedicated to all those companies who paid thousands of dollars to avoid the Y2K catastrophe.) © 23:59:59 December 31, 1999.

Professor de Piano

"I met a man in the neighbourhood who said he could give music lessons to the twins. His name is Wolfgang Gerhard."

"That would be nice. They <u>should</u> have lessons. After all, we have a piano and only I play," said my mother. My brother and I had tried the piano some years ago but mama never had the patience to teach us theory, or to ensure that we practiced.

She and papa were in our kitchen. He had been reading his newspaper, as he did every evening before we ate, while mama would prepare her latest creation. She was a good cook and liked to be creative, especially now that she had bought a new recipe book entitled, "Foods of the World". It was a beautiful hardcover book with a picture of a succulent steak garnished with onions, peppers and broccoli on the cover. They asked us what we thought about taking lessons and we agreed that we should try to learn music. After all, music was always playing in our home. Our parents loved listening to classical music, especially those works that featured the piano. We loved it when my mother played and I recall that my favourite piece was the Waltz in A Flat Major Opus 39. One day perhaps I would play that piece too, I used to think.

The next day my father walked with us to the man's house and knocked on the door. After a few moments an older, balding man with rimless spectacles opened it.

"Good morning *Senhor*. You want music lessons for the twins, *ja?*"

He asked us in and we stood inside the door while papa discussed the cost of the lessons and paid the man for the first month. He apologized to the piano teacher for not being able to stay to witness our first lesson.

"Come in *meninos*," he said, as he led us into an adjoining room.

There was a faint medicinal odour in the home. It appeared to come from the kitchen, but could have come from the teacher's dark suit, the pockets of which may have been carrying his medication. The rooms were large and there was little light in the home, other than that from one window which was framed by blue velvet drapes. At the upper right hand corner of the window I noticed a spider's web and a fly struggling to escape. The spider could not be seen.

"We must begin our lesson," he said, ignoring the doomed insect. He sat at the piano and began to play *The French Children's Song*. We had heard it before; many times, since it was one of the pieces my mother played. He turned towards us and looked at me with eyes that seemed to pierce my forehead and drill deep into my brain. With a feeble attempt at a smile, *Senhor* Gerhard offered us a small bowl of sweets. We each took one and put it in our pockets to eat later.

A silver candelabra on the piano held five long white candles. A Turkish rug covered a portion of the plank floor, and freshly cut flowers in a crystal vase, stood in the centre of a rosewood table. These furnishings did little to allay the coldness of the house which had the ambiance of a hospital lobby. Oil paintings hung on the walls. I assumed these were originals, since the couple appeared to have expensive tastes. The paintings had a common theme. There was a man, or a woman, in these paintings, but each artwork featured the adults with twin children. None were smiling. The eyes of the adults and children were expressionless. They appeared to be corpses, or perhaps people with a terminal illness, hanging on to the last moments of life. I sensed that the house harboured dark secrets.

I began to feel cold in this dark dismal room and my fingers began to tremble. Perhaps this man had invited us to be his students for another reason. His apparent fascination with twins.

"I see you like my paintings." He interrupted my thoughts as my brother fingered the keys nervously.

"Yes *Senhor*. I like to paint too." I stammered.

"Perhaps you will be a great painter one day, or maybe you will become an accomplished pianist, *ja?*"

He watched us while he played, like any teacher would. But he did not appear to be listening, and was more intent at gazing at our faces. It was uncanny. I was uncomfortable, as was Roberto.

"Some juice for you boys?" his wife asked after she entered the room and placed two crystal tumblers of guava juice on the rosewood table.

When I sat on the piano bench the teacher closed the drapes and allowed only a shaft of sunlight through. It silhouetted his form as he sat with his back to the window and observed me. In his hand he held a small notebook and began to sketch while he beckoned me to play a scale. My fingers trembled and did not strike the notes correctly. He asked me to restart the scale.

"How old are you?"

"Eight," answered Roberto quickly. Perhaps too quickly, showing his nervousness in being in this home with the man who never smiled.

"Your eyes," he said "are unlike each other. That is very unusual." He continued to sketch as he spoke. "Do you know who Wagner is?" We replied that we believed he was a composer.

"When you get better, I will teach you some of his music."

He gave us lessons for the summer and then he disappeared. Papa had gone to his home but it was up for sale. The immediate neighbours did not know when the couple had left, since they had never spoken to them.

"Very strange that he would leave without telling me" said my father. "He didn't even take the last month's money for the lessons. Did he say anything to you Joao, Roberto?"

"No papa," we answered.

That was a long time ago and I had forgotten about him. On June 6, 1985 I had laid flowers on the graves of my parents at the *Embu das Artes* cemetery in Sao Paulo. As I followed the path leading out of the cemetery I noticed a pile of soil near one of the older graves. The gravestone had been turned over, and there were police surrounding the grave, as the coffin was being removed.

Some days later I opened the newspaper. On page seven was a small black and white picture. I looked at it closely and recognized the piano teacher from my childhood. I read the article beneath the photograph and it stated that the West German government had refused to accept the remains of their former citizen.

The dark eyes and the unsmiling face were those of Dr. Josef Mengele.

The Unholy Family

Rain washed away the blood that trickled from the young boy's mouth and ears, as he lay on the cobbled street. The passengers disembarked from the bus that had just run over him. Many of them were screaming hysterically, others gazing in silent shock with their hands on their mouths. Some were on their cell phones calling the police. I knelt by the child and anointed his forehead and administered the Last Rites while he gradually drifted away. It was hard. For me, and especially for the many women who had dismounted from the bus. They acted as if it was their own nine-year-old child who now lay there lifeless. I consoled as many as I could, while the police questioned the driver and other witnesses.

"Monsignor, did you see what happened?"

"He appeared to have tripped," I answered.

"How?" the officer asked me.

"I'm not sure," I said, wiping the rain from my eyes, "but he was standing next to me and stepped onto the street and tripped."

"Do you know him?"

"Yes," I said, "his name is Giovanni Gambino. He is an altar boy and served at my Mass this morning."

I continued to answer further questions as the officer took notes while another held an umbrella over us, as the rain fell like sheets from the blackening sky. A siren sounded and flashing blue lights pierced the fog in the square as an ambulance arrived. *"Tomorrow I will say a Mass for his soul,"* I thought to myself as the body was put on a gurney, while mothers wailed. A new bus driver had taken the place of the other, who was trembling in shock in the police car close to us.

"Thank you Monsignor. If you remember anything more, please call me." He gave me his card and I nodded and walked away. I suddenly felt tired. Very tired. How many more deaths, like this one, must there be?

Later that evening I watched the orange orb of the sun sink behind the dome of the basilica. I had witnessed many sunrises and sunsets in my seventy-six years, and knew that there were not too many left for me to enjoy. Perhaps tomorrow I would make my confession. I would tell my confessor that I was negligent and a child lost his life because of that. The letter is a detail I do not need to mention at the confessional. Why should I? It could have been a fraudulent letter. I turned on the lamp on my writing desk in the apartment and read the letter again. My understanding of the significance was exactly as it was when I first read it, after Giovanni had given it to me early this morning, before Mass. I knew his father very well. He had worked with us for over four decades and was trusted by all to take care of his most important master, which he did admirably. He even tasted his master's food to ensure that it had not been poisoned. That, unfortunately, was his undoing. I opened the letter. It was dated July 17, 1963.

My dearest Giovanni,

You are reading this letter because I am already dead. I wish your mother was alive to read this instead of you. Have faith, my son.

You know how much I loved my work, but I never told you about the angry murmurings I had heard in the corridors, some weeks after the election. 'How can these men be angry at someone so good, so honest, and so loved by so many?' I asked myself often. When I entered his chambers he always smiled at me and asked me about you. He listened with so much interest. He asked me if I liked the food that was cooked for him. I was his Food Taster among my other duties. It was only in the last few months that I noticed the soup had a metallic taste. I assumed this was because of the new plumbing that had been installed in the kitchen, so I never questioned it.

When I first had stomach pains I told him about it. He consoled me in his loving way and said not to worry, that it is part of aging, and he had stomach pains too. It was only a few weeks ago, after he died, that I knew what may have happened. But it was too late for me.

My dearest Giovanni, my master may have been poisoned, as I was. It is very unlikely that we both got similar pains at the same time. His doctors attended to him but I did not visit our Dr. Marcello until it was too late. When I finally did, he asked me to have some tests and this confirmed that I was in the final stages of cancer and that I should make my peace with God. I didn't tell you this. I know how difficult it would have been for you to know that I would be leaving you so soon. Especially since your grandfather lived until he was ninety-one, and your grandmother until she was ninety-eight.

Please, my son, take this letter to someone you can trust. He will make sure that the truth will be known. Goodbye my little one. You have a great life ahead of you. With your guardian angel, your mother and I will always watch over you.

Love and God bless,

Papa.

There was no doubt as to what I had to do. The accusation could destroy the foundations of our organization. I ripped the letter and twisted the halves together. The match in my fingers burst into flame and I lit the white candle on my desk. Carefully I placed the letter in the flame and watched as it was consumed. The words therein were now only smoke, spiralling slowly to the ceiling. I was puzzled however, because the smoke curling to the ceiling was <u>black</u> and not <u>white</u> as I had expected from this type of paper. Was Satan in the room with me watching what I was doing? Was he waiting for me to enter the Gates of Hell? Perhaps. But then again, maybe I hadn't <u>intentionally</u> pushed the boy and caused his death. My memory plays tricks on me sometimes.

A picture of me as a young altar boy was on my desk. My youthful smile conveyed the enthusiasm and exuberance of being part of the great Catholic Church. I had participated in early Masses on chilly winter mornings, while others lay dreaming in their warm beds. Then there was Midnight Mass at Christmas, when the bells tolled and resonated with my joyful heart. I had been entranced by the orange glow of the twelve candles on the altar, and the warm scent of beeswax as the flame burned silently in the peace and tranquility of the cathedral. And my nose still smelled the fruity aroma of freshly made wine, which I believed would turn into the blood of Christ after it was consecrated. And the sweet smell of incense as the congregation was blessed, nodding and murmuring prayers for their salvation, as the smoke curled and kissed their faces. All these memories from my childhood returned as I looked into the eyes of that innocent boy in the photograph.

The innocent boy who grew up and became the monster that I am now. One who had consoled hundreds at funerals, who had listened attentively at Confession, and forgiven so many sinners over all those years. And now who did what needed to be done, just to protect our great institution. But now one who has lost his innocence. I do regret however, the loss of Paulo and Giovanni Gamboni when the only victim was supposed to be Angelo Roncalli, known to all as Pope John XXIII. He was a man who belonged to another time, but not our time. But then, it may have been part of God's plan and I am only a humble servant in the Family. But the Family I belong to cannot be destroyed due to the ramblings of one dying man. Our Family is too important to me and I had to protect them.

Wouldn't you have done the same?

A Brush with the Beasts

I'm telling you this in confidence. She had goaded me into this. I should have known that, and could have avoided this mess. But then, I had to prove that I was a man. A real man. But the job that I was about to take on, was for a much younger, aggressive type of individual which I am not.

It was getting late as I walked silently to the side of the house. I held the knife in my hand and readied myself for the job. Was I up to the task? The liquid in the gallon can was likely enough to leave no trace or evidence of a previous, badly executed task. For years and years, I had tolerated it but I couldn't stand it anymore. There was always another reason why I should not act, but now the time had passed and what needed to be done, was going to get done today. There was no chance that I would not act now, no matter what the danger was.

I carefully opened the gate, hoping that the animals wouldn't hear me. The gate closed behind me and I began climbing the ladder to the window clutching the shaft with the shiny, sharp blade in my right hand. I had reached the third rung when suddenly an animal leaped on my back, claws digging deeply into my shoulder. There was little I could do, since I held the gallon can in one hand, and the knife and an upper rung with the other. More beasts looked up from below ready to join their partner. I swung the gallon can around my back and hit the creature. It snarled and dropped off my shoulders, its claws leaving deep scratches on my back.

Climbing to the higher rung, I was able to work on the window, slowly and carefully using my blade to dislodge the dirt that prevented it from opening. I opened the can, the lid of which I had loosened earlier. A generous amount was used and I began climbing down, swinging the closed can in large arcs to keep the attackers at bay. Without turning my back on them, I opened the second gate and stepped in. I was standing on something soft, but I couldn't see it in the shadows. I hoped it wasn't a body. The smell was unmistakeable. A large shepherd leapt at me and I dropped the can and all its contents. It had a large pink object in its mouth and thankfully had not dropped it. I looked at the soles of my shoes. Shit! That's what it was. Clothes dripping with the liquid and shit on my shoes!

I was not looking forward to the next time I had to paint the windows, with the cats and dogs showing their affection for me.

The Meeting-by Accident

November the twenty-fifth was a day which I will never forget. The day that I was smitten. It was an experience like no other. You may not believe it, and I too, sometimes doubt that it happened to me. I can still feel the emotion and the pain of the accident, as if it had occurred just yesterday.

It had been a cold and bitter season in Toronto, unusual for the city which often saw Autumn linger on. On that day, November twenty-fifth, the cold bit deep as I entered the subway station at Yonge and Bloor.

I remember an older woman lugging her suitcase up the stairs, puffing and panting. I stopped and offered to help her, but she shook her head and smiled. A smile from an old wizened face, with wrinkles carved around eyes that had seen Toronto as it was in the fifties. Waspish and intolerant of foreigners, especially those from Eastern Europe. I knew, since my father was part of the flood of immigrants from that part of the world. He had been beaten up regularly in the schoolyard for being a newcomer from a poorer country. But that was Toronto then, but is not Toronto now, a far more welcoming city. *Tough lady* I thought as she passed me, but she had to be tough to be riding the subway so close to midnight. I noticed something yellow fluttering down the stairs and thought it was a yellow ribbon she had used to mark her luggage, so I asked:

"Is this yours?" Then I saw that it was remnants of police tape.

"Probably from accident, yesterday. Very sad," she replied. The accent could have been Hungarian, or Romanian.

"Too much people on platform. Too much pushing for train," the woman said as she hefted her bag onto the mezzanine and continued up the stairs, before being swallowed by the darkness above.

I climbed down into the dimly lit bowels of the subway station. *Into the Valley of Death*, I recalled from poetry I had learned as a child. The platform was deserted and I could hear the diminishing rumble of the train that had just departed into the tunnel to my left. *Shit! I missed it. Now I'll have to wait another fifteen minutes for the next one!* Fumbling in my pocket I pulled out my iPod. *May as well listen to my audiobook.* I shoved the buds into my ear and scrolled through the Library and found *"After Darkness."* I resumed listening to the story.

There was a muffled cry coming from the attic. Her damp palm tightened on the banister, knuckles white with tension. Her face drained of blood. "Oh God! Is it back?" she asked herself. The voice droned on, as I leaned against the white tiled wall, which was more like a headstone. *Cold and lifeless like a mausoleum* I thought. I squinted into the shadowy tunnel hoping the train would arrive sooner and noticed a bench on my left. It was under the clock that read 11.55 p.m. *Five minutes to midnight and then ten more for the stupid train!*

I ambled over but noticed, as the area became slightly brighter, that someone was sitting on the bench whom I hadn't noticed before. It appeared to be a young girl with a knee-length purple coat and black boots. I hesitated for a moment and looked at her, expecting her to turn the other way with the universal gesture that she did not want to be spoken to. *She may think I'm going to hit on her* I thought. Instead she turned to me, looked up and smiled. I was not invading her space. She said something but I couldn't hear because my earphones were continuing with the story: *And it gripped her neck constricting her fragile gullet.*

"Sorry," I said, as I pulled the ear buds out.

"You just missed it," she said. The platform light gave a bluish pallor to her face. *They've got to put better lighting in these stations. I hate mercury vapour lamps. It's a deathly light.* I thought.

"I didn't notice you here earlier. Did you come in after me?" I asked.

"Seems like I've been here all night." She pulled her collar together with her finely formed hands as the cold air from the street crept down the stairwell. Her hands looked as pale as a slab of marble. *She must be anemic* I thought. *Can't just be the light.* I put my iPod back into my pocket and looked at her again. She was very pretty, but appeared so fragile and so melancholy. I had the urge to hug her and to comfort her. Perhaps it would put some colour back into her bloodless cheeks.

"I'm Emily. Worked late tonight James?" She held out her hand which I grasped gently. I noticed that her fingers were very cold and damp as if she had just been playing with snow. I was startled that she knew my name since I seldom forget a face especially one like this, with dark hair framing an angelic smile. *Had I left my office badge on?* I looked down but it wasn't. "It was on the iPod," she giggled.

"Your eyesight must be extremely good to see an engraving in this light."

"Eyes are still good; despite all the cramming I'm doing. Exam is tomorrow. English Lit."

"English Lit?" I asked. "Figures."

"What do you mean?" she asked.

"Emily. Emily Bronte and English Lit. Go together," I responded sagely.

"No. Emily <u>Smith</u>. The other one is dead. Long since," she laughed.

"It would be hard to find you in the phone book I guess. Bronte would have been easier. U. of T.?" I asked.

"Yes, final year, thank God. Hope I can find a job after that. Not enough work for someone with an Arts degree. Been moonlighting as a waitress to pay my way through school. Have a big student loan to pay off when I graduate."

She suddenly radiated a warmth which drew me closer to her. My feelings were not of attraction which was not an uncommon feeling for me at age thirty. Instead I felt the urge to protect her. She was in her early twenties and really quite good looking, but my feelings for her were more fraternal. *What is it about this poor girl whom I want to take home...to keep warm, to look after?*

"Things were much easier when I graduated," I said lightly, hoping she hadn't read my mind.

I felt guilty that I had graduated from Osgoode Hall, a respected school for Law students in Toronto. I was with one of the better firms on Bay Street specializing in Criminal Law and was earning a very good salary. But here was this little sparrow sitting in a cold, dark subway station, after possibly having worked for eight dollars an hour at a mediocre restaurant. *Probably has twenty dollars from tips in her pocket,* an amount I had spent for a couple of drinks after work the previous evening.

"When I graduated they were even hiring Grade Tenners. Management positions you know. Those guys rise quickly in the company,"

I joked. My laugh echoed eerily off the tiled walls, as if we were in a crypt. We continued to make small talk. I liked her, and could tell she was very comfortable talking to me. No other persons were on the platform, and even if they were, I would not have noticed them because this little creature had captivated me. Nothing else seemed to matter at the time. I hoped that the train would be late. I wanted to be with her. I needed to care for her. To protect her. As I drew closer to her I smelled roses.

"My phone number," she said.

"What?" I asked.

"You wanted my phone number." She took out her iPhone and the blue LED display sparkled in her eyes.

"It's Wednesday. Your phone says 'Tuesday'," I said.

Suddenly, she raised her hand to her mouth.

"Wednesday?!" she screamed, eyes widening.

"What's wrong? Are you OK?" I asked as I clutched her shoulders. Inexplicably I was overcome with a deep sadness when I touched her. She lowered her hand and opened her mouth in a silent scream as if to say "NO….!"

"Emily! What's wrong?" I was now shaking her but could feel little resistance, possibly due to her frail form. An intense white light, reflected in her dilated pupils, grew larger by the millisecond. I looked over my shoulder. The train was coming at full speed, horn screeching like an angry banshee. Brakes had been applied and metal squealed on metal and I was suddenly being dragged under the train! My clothes were shredded and my skin was burning as I saw the sleepers of the track race by my eyes, before the train came to a halt. I turned my head and saw her pale hand, still holding the iPhone with the display showing Tuesday, 11.55 pm. And a text message from Emily: "*C Ya*".

I was fading. Fading fast. And falling. Like into a deep well with black, cold water working its way up to my toes, legs, torso and neck. Then, after some moments, there was a shimmering light on the surface. Waxing and waning. I struggled to breathe. The pain was gone. And the cold. As suddenly as it had come. The blackness, now dissolving into dimness. Faint light now penetrated the shadows above me. From the top of the well I could hear voices. Now shouts. I was being lifted.

"Hey mister, can you hear me?" I looked up. Someone was bending over me shaking my shoulder. My body shook like a stubborn leaf in the wind.

"He's OK. His eyes are open." Urgency in another voice: "we should call an ambulance."

"What happened? Where am I?" I murmured struggling to get up. Someone reached a hand out and helped me. The platform light darkened and brightened as I tried to regain my balance, helping hands holding my shoulders. The three men looked at me cautiously. They were young.

"Are you OK?" one of them asked.

"The train. I was under the train," I said.

"The train won't be here for another 5 minutes. We found you lying near the bench."

"Convulsing," another said.

"What?" I asked. My lips still trembling while my heart palpitated furiously.

"We need to call an ambulance," the guy with the Toronto Blue Jays baseball cap said.

"No, no… I'm OK now," I stammered as the chills overcame me again.

"Are you sure? I have a cell. I can call an ambulance."

"Thanks, I'm fine."

My heart struggled to pump warming blood to my chilly fingers and feet. The platform rumbled and a blast of warm air from the tunnel heralded the arrival of the train. The doors opened and one of the three young men held my shoulder as I entered the car unsteadily. They watched me as I sat down on the first available seat. I felt ice cubes in my hands. That fainting spell had never happened to me before. *Must be a blood sugar thing*, I thought. I smiled weakly at the three Good Samaritans. Two sat across from me and one next to me. They were teenagers. *How nice* I thought. *Young people get such a bad rap these days*. I knew that. I had helped defend some delinquents in the courts.

"You look a lot better now mister," the Blue Jays fan next to me smiled. He turned from me and opened *The Star*.

"Happened here last night. Sad, isn't it?" he asked as he showed me the headline: *Train claims another victim at Sheppard Yonge station.*

I looked more closely at the tabloid. Beneath the headline was a small photo with familiar eyes which smiled up at me. It was Emily. Suddenly I smelled roses, but the scent quickly faded. I had been smitten. Smitten by the ghost of Emily.

Tommy

The Plan:

The caller said I was to meet the man at the *Shamrock and Roll,* a new place in Galway near Claddagh Park, opposite *Connelly's Funeral Home.* It wasn't the best time to be out. A heavy fog had enveloped the roadways and I could barely recognize the shops along *St. Augustine Street,* where this place was supposed to be. Finally, I saw it. Next to *Reagan's Shoe Repair* where I had often had my old leather boots fixed. Good Old Reagan. He also fought for the cause years ago, and finally quit due to his worsening emphysema. I'm sure he would have preferred death by bullets, rather than by emphysema, but in our type of work we needed people who wouldn't get sudden coughing fits when the prey was nearby.

Shamrock and Roll! Only an Englishman would come up with a name like that. I pushed open the door, adjusted my fake beard, and took a quick look left and right, with my hand clutching the weapon in my pocket, as was my habit when I entered unfamiliar places. The pub smelled of fresh paint, instead of stale beer, which I was more accustomed to in establishments where I met my contacts.

The juke box was blaring with Irish music to impress the half dozen tourists who were sitting around some of the low tables drinking our beer. They were singing *Danny Boy* off key, with German intonations. *Heil Hitler!* There was a small dance floor but nobody was dancing. I saw a grandfather clock in one corner and proceeded to the table next to it. This was the spot where I was supposed to meet Tommy. I removed my raincoat, draped it over the chair, and had barely sat down, when I heard a voice.

"Liam?"

"Yes," I said, although that wasn't my name.

"You must be Tommy."

The lad was possibly in his late teens, usually the best age for our new recruits. Age makes you too cautious and less prone to taking risks. I shook his hand and he put both hands around mine, confirming his identity with the prearranged gesture. He then handed me a piece of rock from his pocket and said, "This has a touch of Blarney."

I peered at it closely through the horn-rimmed glasses I used for this special meeting. It was my piece of jade that I had given to the intermediary. These days the other side was infiltrating our group and we couldn't take chances. I ordered a few pints. As we sipped our Guinness, he told me about his previous assignments and how he was looking forward to the hit I had planned for him. I reached into my pocket and showed him the photograph.

"Him?!"

"That's the man," I replied.

"I thought he was already dead."

"He will be, if you do the job right."

Tommy took several gulps from his glass. I looked at the lad in the green squall jacket, with his curly mop of red hair. Young and brash. Could I rely on him? I decided to take my chance because the window of opportunity was closing fast. The tourists were still singing loudly and paid no attention to us. I had my back to them and told Tommy the plan. It had to be on August the twenty-seventh and he had to travel to Mullaghmore and meet with an intermediary at the place I named. He had two weeks to prepare.

We left the pub after I was sure that he understood the details I had given him. Outside the door we parted company. As I watched him being swallowed up by the fog, I had some shadow of doubt that he was the right person for the job. But I had no other options this late in the game.

The Execution:

"Another pint for you laddies?" asked the buxom barmaid as Tommy gulped down the dark foamy fluid, not caring that some of it dripped down the corners of his mouth, and under his frayed collar. He nodded.

"So what's up?" asked Freddy pulling the chair next to his buddy.

"Got plans. Big plans." Tommy lowered his voice.

"You should take a break Tommy, it's only bin four weeks since the last job. You gotta lie low for a while, don't you think?"

"Nah, gotta keep goin'. Stay in practice that way."

"But Tommy. Do you really have to do the job so soon? You'll get caught, laddie. They could be searching for you right now." Freddy looked over his shoulder to see if anyone was sitting nearby.

"Got a really big one."

"What else is new? That's all you do… the big ones."

"This one's a really big one though."

"How big?"

"I'm gonna get Dickie."

"Dickie?"

"Yup, but this one is the big Dickie."

"Big Dickie! You're mad, man! Won't work Tommy. You'll really need more than the luck of the Irish. He has lots of protection."

"Doesn't."

"Does."

"No, I'm sure of it. Checked out by Paddy."

"Who's Paddy?"

"Never mind." Tommy had given too much away already to his young friend.

"Few more pints?" asked the barmaid bending over the table to allow them to peer down her cleavage, as she cleared the tankards off the table. However, there were bigger things on their minds than tits that evening.

"Yup." He answered, as he wiped his mouth with his sleeve.

Some of the regular patrons were starting to leave, pulling on their jackets and snugging up their collars. They cast their glances at Tommy and Freddy, whom they suspected were here to stir up some trouble in Limerick.

"Looks nasty doesn't it?" Tommy said as he paid at the cash register.

"Close to the end of August, whaddya expect? Better be goin' then. We got a train to catch tomorra."

It was August the twenty-sixth and a light rain continued to fall as the train for Mullaghmore pulled into the station at 6.45 p.m. Tommy and Freddy got on and put their knapsacks on the luggage rack above them. Other than a few drunks returning to their villages after their work at the local slaughter house, there were few people in the compartment, which reeked of piss and puke. With a long whistle the train started to move away from the platform.

"Tickets please," asked the conductor. He punched the tickets given to him and asked, "You lads been to Mullaghmore before?"

"Only me. My aunt lives up there. Tommy needs to see a village which is goin' green 'cos of some dedicated tree-huggers."

"Ireland will always be green laddies." The conductor smiled and moved away.

Few words were exchanged as the train continued on. But they would make small talk if a uniformed policeman came into the compartment. They had learned that making eye contact with the cops usually led to some questions being asked. As they approached Mullaghmore, only an older couple remained sitting at the far end of the compartment, out of ear shot. Freddy whispered to Tommy.

"You sure he has no bodyguards?"

"Yup. Feels everyone loves him. Thinks he's a hero."

A little later they were disembarking at the station and began their walk to the station exit. As they approached the exit, a man who was seated on a bench rose to meet them. Tommy slowed down.

"Tommy?"

"Yup that's me. You Paddy?"

"Yes. Thought you'd be alone."

91

"I'm never alone these days. This is Freddy. He watches my back. Besides, travelling alone can look suspicious in these parts."

"There's been a slight change in plans."

"Why?" asked Tommy, searching his knapsack for another packet of cigarettes. He wouldn't have a chance to smoke later.

"Too many tourists in the area. Someone else will operate the remote."

"Who?" Tommy asked as he pulled on his cigarette.

"Not your concern."

They got into Paddy's *Renault* and he drove down a street not far from the dock, and parked the car halfway down the road from *O'Doul's Pub*.

"Looks like a good place. Should get a pint or two before you start work. It's cold and you will be colder in the water," said Paddy.

There were a few young people in the pub speaking loudly. Some tourists could be relied on to advertise their presence. Other than this group, there were no other persons who looked like undercover cops. After quaffing back his pint Tommy rose to leave, putting a few coins on the table.

"You'll find the stuff in the wheel well," said Paddy.

"Be back soon."

He went to the *Renault*, opened the boot which had not been locked, and pulled out the spare tire. A couple of passersby moved past him. He waited, and then removed a large, black knapsack from the wheel well. He hefted it onto his back, closed the boot, and began walking towards the dock. Paddy had described it as a thirty footer boat painted white, with "*Shadow V*" in black on the side. He slowed his pace to appear to be a tired hitch-hiker, and studied each boat he passed. The *Shadow V* was now in view, but he didn't stop or slow down when he passed it, because he saw two figures on board a neighbouring boat, ready to cast off. Tommy continued walking until he found a darker, more protected area near the water. He dropped his sack behind a tree and quickly took out the wet suit and pulled it on in the darkness. Next he removed a floatation collar and the explosive device from the knapsack. He was well acquainted with this device and had used this on other occasions. Light, reliable and very effective. It was encased in a protector which he unzipped so that he could confirm the location of the remote operated receiver switch. He zipped it up again, and placed the collar securely around the device. Tommy entered the water and swam silently to the hull of the *Shadow V* pushing the package in front of him. Nobody was on the decks of any of the nearby boats. He removed the outer protector, placed the magnetic object on a metal portion of the hull, two feet below the water line, and engaged the the remote switch.

"Happy sailing you bastard!" He swam away as the moon rose over Claddagh.

The Prey:

Dickie looked out at the distant surf as the seagulls dove into the emerald water. Then he turned to admire his neatly pressed white trousers, and his white sharkskin jacket, with the naval epaulets. He carefully combed his thinning grey hair. Age had been kind to him he reflected, just as his life had been. A free spirit doing whatever he wanted to do in his privileged life.

"It's a perfect morning for fishing. Want to come with me Nickie boy?"

"Love to grandpa. Can I bring Paul?"

"Sure. Why don't you run ahead and bring him to the boat?" said Dickie.

"Can I come too?" Doreen asked.

"What? An eighty-two-year-old woman wants to go fishing?"

"Now, now. You're not much younger than I am, old man."

"Don't bring your bikini. You wouldn't want to arouse me." He grinned as he packed his suntan oil, swimming trunks and some magazines. "We'll take the Bentley to the dock."

Two men had checked the interior of the *Shadow V* for any vagabonds and had warmed up the engine so that Dickie could set sail immediately.

"All's good sir." They waved and watched him embark with his lady friend. A few minutes later, they greeted the two teenagers who lifted their bicycles onboard. The men pulled the ropes off the capstan. Dickie pointed the nose at the open water and slowly began to increase speed.

I sat in my usual spot with my fishing line in the water, as I had done on most afternoons in the summer. A police car drove by and I waved to them. They knew me as a regular visitor and had come to talk to me sometimes while I fished. It was a nice quiet place farther down from the main dock where the boats were tethered. Dickie usually came here in August even though he knew it was risky. He enjoyed living on the edge. In that way we were alike.

I touched the remote in my pocket to make sure it was still there. As the boat moved into the open water headed towards Donegal Bay, I pressed the button. A muffled roar and a large column of water shot up fifty feet into the air. Pieces of the boat flew skyward and the larger section began to list. The smoking wreck of the *Shadow V* was being swallowed by the roiling waters of the North Atlantic. I dropped the remote into the water, packed up my fishing gear and walked slowly towards the small agitated crowd at the boat dock. I blended well with the many that shook their heads in disbelief at what had befallen this important visitor.

The Finale:

Dickie felt cold, very cold. How did he get into the water? Must have blacked out. He looked up at the cloudless sky and saw Japanese Zeros coming straight at him with their guns blazing. Bombs were also being dropped on his ship! *Where are my gunners?* He looked around. *Where are all my men?*

A few days later, Tommy McMahon was arrested and charged with the murder of Louis Francis Albert Victor Nicholas George, the First Earl of Mountbatten of Burma.

Gerry Adams of Sinn Fein stated: *"What the IRA did to him is what Mountbatten had been doing all his life to other people; and with his war record I don't think he could have objected to dying in what was clearly a war situation."*

And what do I think about all this? I felt sorry for Tommy. He was young. Thinking back, there was hope for him and others. But I look at myself, now nearing seventy years and happy that I was never caught. But then again, sometimes I feel I should have been on board with Dickie, suffering the same fate.

That would have been the only way to blow away all the hatred in my heart.

Fatima's Journey

"We must leave now!" My father was shaking my shoulder.

"It's too early for school papa. I need to sleep," I said, as my eyes adjusted to the early morning light of coastal Libya.

"They are coming. Be quick!" He herded us all towards the car. In the distance I could hear large vehicles rumbling down the road and the sound of what I initially thought was fireworks. I knew then what was happening. My father had warned us of the evil which was now spreading in Libya. Together with my father, mother and little brother, we sped along the small streets of Benghazi.

"Where are we going papa?"

"To the coast. There are boats there to take people away." Along the route there were small groups of people huddled in the roadway who tried to stop our car. My father swerved to avoid them.

"Please take us with you," a young woman implored. I could not look into her eyes. I was too ashamed. But there was no room. I would have loved to have taken them all. But I swear to you, there was no room in our small car. We arrived at the dock, where many people stood in line. Fearful, terrified people, who wanted to escape from the men with the black flags. I saw my father take out a roll of notes and hand it to a Somali when our turn came.

"This is not enough for a family of four. Give me more, or you can't board." My father protested and the man gave him back the notes and turned to the next family in line. We went to another boat and a Turkish man looked at me and my brother.

"How old are your children?"

"The boy is four and my daughter is twelve." He nodded and took the money and we began our journey. A flight once again, from a menace that was swarming our lands.

One year has passed since we left Libya where my father worked as an engineer in an oil refinery in Benghazi. We had to leave Syria one year earlier when the men with the black flags began entering Aleppo, my birthplace and that of my parents. They had painted a sign on our door.

"What does the sign mean papa?" I had asked.

"Fatima, this is a sign for us to leave by the morning. It is too dangerous to stay any longer."

"Why papa?" I asked.

"I heard that they did bad things to people at Kilis when they didn't leave, after they had warned them to do so. I cannot tell you what they did my child. You are too young to understand how evil men can be."

My father had told me earlier that there are few countries in the Middle East where Christians were not persecuted. The *Wahabi* sect's beliefs had spread beyond Saudi Arabia where some fundamentalist *mullahs* preached hatred. They encouraged violence against other Muslims who did not share their ultra-orthodox version of Islam. Non-Muslims who would not convert to Islam were labelled as 'Infidels'. Syria was one of the few countries where we had lived in relative peace. Our neighbourhood had Muslim, Jewish and Christian homes and we all lived in harmony and celebrated Eid, Hanukah and Christmas with all our friends. Until the day when the men with the black flags arrived. And now we were fleeing Libya too, with Turkey as our destination.

The boat brought us to Istanbul, where we were allowed entry to a refugee camp, where there were hundreds of people. But, after a few days, we were told to leave the camp. Many others were coming so we had to make place for them. Our small family began our trek north with a large group of people. But we could no longer keep up with the group for very long. My mother had difficulty walking. When she was young she had broken her right ankle and it had not been set properly. She was often in pain. My father thought that if we lagged behind, someone with a lorry or a car would see my mother limp, and perhaps give us a ride. But leaving the safety of the group proved to be a mistake.

Just outside Korlu, three men appeared suddenly from a copse of trees. I was fearful when one of them took out a large knife. How would my father defend us? He was not a street fighter. He was an intelligent man who would talk his way out of conflicts with a reasoned and unemotional approach. He took out some money.

"How much do you want?"

"All the money that you have." A bearded one responded, drawing closer to my father.

My father told them that he needed to keep some money for the long journey ahead. He offered them a few notes. One of the men laughed and hit him hard on the side of the head. He fell to the ground and another man pulled the wad of bills out of his wallet. The man who had hit him stabbed him repeatedly.

"Run!" He cried to us, as blood began to pool beneath him. But we couldn't leave papa. The men told us that if we didn't, they would kill all of us. Mama screamed and tried to pull my father away, but the men began to hit her. One of them grabbed my little brother by his hair and held a knife to his throat.

"Do you want me to kill your son now, or are you going to leave?" He snarled as he pushed Joseph towards my mother. "Run now before we change our minds." He shoved us down the path and we stumbled away until we could no longer hear our father's cries of pain. Mama stopped to go back, but then turned around. She held Joseph's hand and put her other hand on my shoulder.

"It is no use Fatima. He is gone. He is now in the comforting arms of our Holy Mother."

We stopped under a large cedar and I cried with my mother until no more tears came. My father was my guide, my teacher and my inspiration. He loved me as much, if not more, than my mother. I could not believe that one of the pillars of my life had now fallen. How would I cope? How would we cope? My mother totally depended on him. This could not be happening. This must be a nightmare. I know I will wake up and he will be there, smiling down at me. Telling me that he had warm bread and jam ready before I left for school. My mother's voice broke through my thoughts.

"We must continue Fatima. Maybe there will be some good people who may help us. Maybe there are more good men like your father."

She rose, held our hands, and limped towards the roadway. After some minutes of walking along the road, we heard a vehicle behind us. It was a lorry carrying a load of fruits and vegetables. The driver stopped and told us to sit in the front seat. He was an older man. Mostly bald, but with grey hair circling the back of his head. He smiled at me and Joseph and displayed his *paan* stained teeth. He spat the red juice out of his window and turned to my mother.

"I can take you and your children to the next village. They will give you some food. The young ones must be very hungry. It is a difficult road to walk." My mother thanked him and we drove in silence until we arrived at the village. He let us out and gave us some apples and carrots and some money.

"*Allah* be with you for your journey," he said before his lorry rumbled away.

Along the side of the road we found a plastic bottle which we would fill with water later. For many days we walked and walked. Sometimes people passing us on the road would stop and give us some money, food or water. Some would drive us to the next village. Most would just drive by without looking at us. They had likely passed many others like us, who had fled their homes. We were the new homeless pariahs. Too many of us for the locals to care about.

Sometimes we would get a ride in a bus or a lorry. We walked for many, many days along a northern route and arrived in Sofia. Border troops allowed us to stay in a tent city for some days. But then an official came to the camp and told us that the United Nations would not give them enough money. They had no funds to buy food for us. They put us all in lorries to take us to the border with Romania and gave us some biscuits and dried meat for the journey.

After we were dropped off on a roadway in a village, we stopped to eat. Mama nibbled at her food as she had been doing now for several days. Dark shadows encircled her eyes, which had lost their luminescence some days after papa died. Her skin hung from her bones and her movements were slow. I had watched her age quickly. I could not bear to look too long at her. I knew that she was wasting away.

"Here," she said, giving us a piece of *chapatti*, "eat this. I am not hungry."

I knew this was not true but mama refused to eat anymore. She told us that we were growing and needed to eat more than she did. We trekked at night when it was cooler and slept in the day in the woods. We arrived at the border with Hungary, but there was a barbed wire fence and signs in a language I did not understand. But I knew it must have meant "Keep Out", or "Danger", or "Guard Dogs", like so many signs we had seen before in English or Arabic.

And then I saw the poppies. Large, vibrant, red poppies, which I had seen near our home in Aleppo. There were thousands of them in the ditches, beckoning to me as they were ushered by the west wind. Symbols of peace. And hope. Hope is all I have now. When I was eight years old my hope was to become a doctor, and to work in the large hospital in Aleppo. I had been there when my brother was born. The people were so kind to us, especially the doctor who said to me: 'You are a lucky young girl to have such a handsome brother.'

I remember him so well. He was a small man with a big smile that brightened the dark little room in the hospital. He had said his name was Doctor Ahmed. A Muslim name. So many good Muslims in Aleppo before the men with the black flags arrived. That seems like so long ago when I lived in a city which had the Citadel of Aleppo. The jasmine bushes which bordered this beautiful castle had been shredded by gunfire. The acrid fumes of cordite now replaced the dulcet perfume of those small white flowers. The bones of my countrymen now lay in heaps of rubble, where once a magnificent people stood proudly at this Citadel, which overlooked the homes of their beloved.

I looked again at the poppies which continued to bow their heads, seeming to coax us to come through the barbed wire fence. But then a group of young boys began throwing stones at us, so we had to retreat from the border. We continued our journey away from the barbed wire fence of that country that didn't want us.

We have lost our homes and cannot return to our country of birth. We are not welcome anywhere else. There are thousands of us. Nameless, faceless people. Displaced persons. Undesirable refugees. Nowhere to go. Nowhere to hide. Always unwelcome. Some of us will die along the road; others will die in the ocean. The 'lucky' ones will live in tent cities for most of their lives, eating rationed food behind barbed wire fences. Each day, more of their self-esteem will be consumed. Some care about us but most don't.

Mama says she is in pain and needs to rest. She lies down in the ditch. She closes her eyes, hugging my little brother and me. I hear someone running towards us. It is a man with a beard. We must hide.

I try to awaken mama but she won't wake up.

The Mentor

You may not notice me as I walk by you on the streets of Ottawa. I look like any other senior citizen. Sandstone buildings in this city harbour many secrets, best left undisturbed in the musty archives, deep in the basements. But in my case, there are others who know my secret. Others who matter a lot to me, who feel that my actions let down the team. My back is no longer straight as it once was, but is stooped, not only with age, but with a load which I cannot carry anymore. You see, they say I am my brother's keeper and regretfully those deadly sins are shared by me. How long can I carry this cross, this grief, this black stain that has darkened my body and my spirit, more than any other event in my life? I need to confess and I will do so to you.

Now. Before I die.

It all began twenty-five years ago when I was recruiting for the company. An organization of young idealistic men and women, who wanted to change the world for the better. We older ones know that the idealistic spirit is often lost as the years go by. I, for one, know this for certain, when I reflect upon that event a quarter of a century ago.

He was next in line. A young, smart looking individual who was perhaps twenty years old. His bright blue eyes sparkled with the innocence of the young son I once had, who was lost in the war in Afghanistan. His manner, although shy, was not unusual for those who met me for the first time. I admit, I can appear to be an intimidating person, projecting a power that some of us are born with, and some acquire with rigorous training. In my case it was the latter.

"Well young man," I said, "I see from your application that you were born in England and moved to Canada when you were a little boy. You also grew up in Chalk River. What did your father do?"

100

"He worked for Atomic Energy Canada, sir. He was a researcher in the nuclear demonstration plant at Chalk River," he said, holding my gaze briefly.

"Did you not want to follow in your father's proud footsteps by working in that renowned facility? Perhaps become a researcher like he was?"

"He was my stepfather, sir. My parents were divorced shortly after we moved to Canada."

"Oh, I see. And what did your biological father do?"

"He was a metallurgist sir."

"Ah, and that is why your school certificate shows honours in chemistry."

"I liked chemistry sir, but I also did well in math and physics."

"I see that too. Math and physics, eh? I thought you may have liked geography too. You have expressed an interest in travelling, which would be very important in your career with us."

"Yes, sir. I especially like to fly. The farther and faster, the better," he smiled.

The interview lasted no longer than half an hour. He was a good candidate and was the type of recruit we needed. Bright, bold, athletic and venturesome. A month later he had joined us and, as I expected, he was a rapid learner and was close to the top of his class in every subject. I nurtured him as he climbed up the ranks, and guided him towards opportunities that would help his career develop faster. All the reports I had about him had been positive. I often bragged that I was the one that hired him and was his mentor.

However, in retrospect, I should have suspected there was a flaw in his character when he showed so much interest in my twelve-year-old grand-daughter. He always brought her candy and paid special attention to her, when she was with us. Little did I know that deep within him, a satanic obsession was being nurtured.

After I retired, I saw his name in the paper. I almost choked on my toast at breakfast that morning when I read the account of what he had done. My rage, as I read the story, grew to the point that I threw my mug of coffee against the stone fireplace. It shattered and startled my little Scottie who wagged his tail and came over to me to see what was wrong.

I put the paper down and sighed. It was fortunate that I had not caught him, because what I would have done to him would not have been pretty. I would have killed him with my bare hands if I had the chance. I too, was trained as he had been. That bastard had disgraced me. That son of a bitch had fooled me from the start. To think that I trusted him. Gave him all those chances to develop and instead, he played games like the devil, and brought dishonour to me and our organization!

What am I saying? Have I forgotten what he did to his victims? Isn't it far worse than what he has done to me and the organization? Have I become like him? Would I have done the same things he had done, if I had the charm, skill and the opportunity? Don't all of us in the company have that overwhelming urge to exert our power over the enemy? Or the prey? Are we all the same? God forgive me for this. I am a tortured soul and I feel that I too, am responsible for the crimes he has committed. It was I who should have recognized the demon within him. It was I who was in a position to exorcise this demon, to mould his character so that he could have become the man whom I wanted him to be. Honourable. Dedicated. Loyal. Faithful. And most of all a protector of the vulnerable. All the training I had in psychology and leadership should have helped me recognize his true character. I failed. Miserably.

A month later I was asked to attend the formal ceremony. Normally one is honoured to attend a formal ceremony, where your superiors are present to hand out awards. This one was different. Very different.

First a Major pulled out my former protégé's three uniforms from a black garbage bag, placed it in a trash can, added gasoline and flung a burning match into it. The flames quickly turned the uniforms into black smoke which curled up and darkened the bright sun. I was sure I had smelled his odious bodily fluids as they were carried up and away. The stench permeated my own clothing as if he would infect me with his vile disease. His medals were then taken and I watched with seething rage, as these were ground up in a large metal grinder, that screeched and gasped, as it tried to destroy forever any honours that had been bestowed on the man.

His official vehicle was then taken to be crushed. A man who had dishonoured his country, his uniform and all who served with him, and for him. And the disgrace went upwards through the organization, to all those who were instrumental in putting him in a position of trust and respect. I am the guiltiest of them all. I had recruited him. I had mentored him. All the burning, grinding and crushing would never remove the stain he had left on my soul, and the company where he served as the head of our most important strategic asset.

You will not see me walking the streets of Ottawa anymore. No longer can I tolerate the glares, the stares and the unspoken words of my former colleagues and superiors, when I visit the Legion. I am sure they feel I must pay the price. I have made a decision and I believe it to be an honourable one. For I am responsible for creating that monster who became a Colonel.

It is late at night when I write this letter. I am going to my cabinet now, and will remove my military issue pistol. There is one bullet in it. For a special occasion.

This is it.

The Light at the End of the Tunnel

I had been getting weaker and weaker, and knew that there was not much time left. From the metal table I was lying on, I could see the implements which would be used, and shuddered that my end should require these.

I looked back on my life and wondered if there was more that I could have done. It is indeed an odd feeling at times like this, to think about happier times, and whether I could have done things differently. I knew this day would come. But it had come too soon. My wife knew. I had to tell her. But I hadn't told my three children. How could I tell them something like this? My father had never told me about his condition. Neither had my mother. They are gone now.

My thoughts were interrupted by someone groaning on the other side of the wall. The person was obviously in distress. There were gasps and gurgles and occasional mutterings as the labours continued. The clang of instruments in the tray rang through the corridor. Was this the poor soul's last moments? I heard the door of the adjacent room open with a loud click. Before it closed I heard a woman's voice ask, "Is it over now? Poor man. He was so frightened. I'll go and tell his wife."

"No, let me do it," said the doctor, "this is best left to me." Oh God! I thought. Is the guy finished already? I had only heard him a few moments ago and he's already done? And I was next on the list...

I remembered the last time that I was in a hospital. A place where nobody smiled, or laughed. Instead, people with grim faces had stood at the entrance, and those with grimmer faces had left the hospital. What a terrible place to be in. I had promised myself that I would never be in a position where I was left to the mercy of medical staff. I had led a healthy life, but my day of reckoning had finally arrived. How would I be judged for my sins, after all these years on earth?

I was starting to feel dizzy, even though I was lying down. Unusual, I thought. But then again, vital organs can fail at any moment. My pulse was weakening and I tried to call out, but no sound came from my parched throat. I lifted my arm, to grab one of the metal instruments in a tray beside my bed. I wanted to strike the tray to sound an alarm, but was unable to reach it. My heart was now palpitating, and there appeared to be little time left for me.

At that moment the door opened, and a man in a white lab coat entered my room. Thank God, I thought. Help is at hand! But then I saw the light. A brilliant white light, which seemed to get brighter by the minute. Others had told me of this near-death experience but, despite that, it was still terrifying. They had told me that I would be calm, and that I would walk out in peace and tranquility. Into the light. Others would be there, waiting for me on the other side. How much time did I have left, before the inevitable? I dared not think, but looked at the light getting ever brighter. The doctor whispered something to me and moved my hand away from my eyes. But then I felt a sharp pain and was sure it was the end. The light was gone now. All I could sense were the convulsions of my weakened body, as I adjusted to the last moments. Why did I not take care of myself? I asked. It was too late now. The journey through the tunnel was over. My eyes had been squeezed shut but now I opened them, and peered at the man in a white coat, with a smile on his face.

"Dr. Livingstone," I said, "I presume you know that this is the last time I will subject myself to a colonoscopy."

56314701R00063

Made in the USA
Charleston, SC
17 May 2016